THE LEGENDS OF REGIA

BLOOD LOCK

A NOVEL

TENAYA JAYNE

COLD FIRE PUBLISHING LLC

This is a work of fiction. Names, characters, places, and incidents are products of the author's imagination or are used fictitiously and are not to be construed as real. Any resemblance to actual events, locales, organizations, or persons, living or dead, is entirely coincidental.

Cover Art created by Erika Doucesse

Edited by Amanda Fiske & Valerie Hatfield

Proofread by Ally Robertson

COLD FIRE PUBLISHING, LLC

All Rights Reserved

OTHER BOOKS BY TENAYA JAYNE

Forbidden Forest

Forest Fire

Verdant

Dark Soul

Burning Bridges

Blue Aspen

PROLOGUE

Shreve gasped, waking suddenly from a deep sleep. He clutched at his chest as his heart turned into a clock. The thumping tissue now kept time, counting down. Desperation ran cold and constant, just under his skin. He didn't have much life left to live. The knowledge that he was dying slid easily inside him like the blood in his veins. Was it real? How did he know for sure his body would soon begin to shut down?

He couldn't answer. He just knew.

He blinked and rubbed his face. His hands moved methodically over the planes of the bone structure. It wasn't the right one. It wasn't *his* face.

He lay back and gazed at the Bellis stone ceiling of his Kyhael apartment. It was time to move on. He'd lived as an elf for months. From the very first day, he knew it wasn't the right fit, but he wanted to stay close to Rahaxeris. Not that Rahaxeris knew he was there. Or perhaps he did. There wasn't much Rahaxeris didn't know. But since he wasn't going to make contact with the *Rune-dy,* there was no point in him staying any longer in Kyhael. It had been a good place for him to keep his ear to the ground.

He'd learned Forest was now revered as the savior, since Copernicus had died by her hand. There were wild rumors since she'd had her child. No one had seen her. She'd made no public appearances.

Some believed her to have died in childbirth. He listened to all the gossip, but he didn't put much stock in any of it. Forest was alive, he was sure of it.

He didn't need to worry about her. She didn't need him, and he needed to focus on his task.

What would he try next? Everything.

So little time, his body warned. He must search harder, faster. What a tragedy it would be if he failed. Always confused, he grappled with the ancient, universal questions of right and wrong. Sometimes wrong was very clear in regard to his bloody memories. His hands were guilty. His heart, however, was still in question.

He got up from the bed and went to the mirror. Copernicus stared back at him. His teeth clenched in anger. It wasn't his face.

Shreve moved his elf DNA to the forefront with only a thought. His features changed accordingly without any other effort on his part. He wasn't just shifting to look like an elf. He *was* an elf, *and* a shifter, ogre, vampire, werewolf, and also wizard. He longed to be just one thing. Because he was everything, he was nothing.

He left the apartment. No one stopped him as he exited through the gates of the city. He traveled light with only one change of clothes and Forest's old silver sword. The morning light kissed his troubled head as he ventured out into the wilderness that stretched out between the clusters of civilization.

Off in the distance, the silhouette of the Lair, the mountain where the werewolves lived, obstructed his view of the sky. He had yet to try to live as wolf. He moved toward the defiant mountain range. It would be where he searched next.

Shreve wasn't searching for the answer to save Regia from the wizards. He was searching for himself. For the moral compass he never had, his own identity, and yes, he searched to find his real face. And that was all he wanted now that he knew he was dying. To know who he really was, before it was all over.

CHAPTER ONE

The warm golden afternoon sunlight stretched through the windowpanes over Forest as she gazed at her baby daughter, sleeping in her arms. Forest felt, as most mothers do, that her baby was the most beautiful ever born. Despite her bias, it was damn near true. Tesla was a breathtakingly beautiful child in spite of her abnormalities. Her tiny baby hands, curled into fists, rested on her chest. The veins in her hands glowed electric red, brightly contrasting against her pale skin. As if her hands were covered with red lace or henna tattoos. When Tesla curled her hand around Forest's index finger, the power that throbbed from the baby was stingingly painful to her.

Aside from her hands, Tesla bore marks on her chest, over her heart. Every time her heart beat, a red glow surged out from her heart and visibly ran up through the veins around it. The red light on her chest looked like the outline of a flower.

The rocking chair creaked rhythmically as Forest ran the tips of her fingers over and over her daughter's cheek and through the silky wisp of black hair on her head. Tesla had Syrus' coloring. Black hair and gray eyes. But her ears were pointed at the top like Forest's, and although her eyes were the same color as her father's, the shape of them was clearly her mother's.

Forest's fear and heartbreak surrounding the distortion inside her daughter didn't hinder her love or the fierce passion she had to protect her child. Tesla owned her heart completely, the moment she was born. And Forest would do everything in her power to help her baby.

Rahaxeris was due any minute now. He came every day to treat the swelling power that throbbed in Tesla's hands. She couldn't stop crying otherwise. She wailed something awful most of the time. Forest cried herself to sleep almost every night because she felt like she was incapable of soothing her child's pain. Forest simply didn't know what to

4

do.

Syrus had it easier with Tesla. She would quiet for him and look directly into his eyes. She would splay her tiny fingers on his skin, his power snapping and dancing with hers. Direct contact with Syrus was the only other thing that seemed to bring relief to the child. Forest hated that she was jealous of the easy connection they had, but she was.

Forest smiled down at Tesla and shook her head. She was already daddy's girl. She marveled, as she did a few times every day, at the fact that she was a mother. It was weird as well when she thought about Syrus being a father. Her powerful, tall drink of water, mage was a father. Yeah... weird.

Four months had passed since Tesla had been born, but still, Forest had yet to actually go back to work. She had healed quickly, within hours of giving birth. Her stomach flattened back out in a week, and her body mostly returned to its previous state, with the exception of her hips, that had gone a bit wider. She wanted to try and work them down originally, but Syrus' response to her changed frame caused her to rethink that. The subtle addition to her figure drove him wild.

A small smile curved the side of Forest's mouth as she thought about him. Life felt too hard, and she didn't think she could have kept her head up if she didn't have Syrus. Something dark and heavy had entered her heart the night Tesla was born. Rahaxeris' look and voice replayed over and over in her mind. *There's something wrong.* From her first day as a mother, her joy, soft and vibrant in the center, had razor edges of pain. She'd never even had the temporary reprieve of denial. All she had to do was look at Tesla to know it was true.

Her daughter was in pain. Would she always be in pain? There was too much magic inside her. It ran wild and rampant through her like a mess of frayed, electrical live wires. Would the abundance slacken as she grew? Would her mind be fractured?

Forest's throat clenched She felt desperate for answers, and terrified at the same time. She hoped all her worry was unneeded. Perhaps Tesla would grow easily, and her physical problems would solve themselves as she matured. Perhaps people would accept her because she was so beautiful and overlook her abnormalities.

Forest would take her sword to the cruelty of the world, if only she could. If only cruelty wasn't often invisible and intangible, she would slash it to death without mercy. Her arms tightened protectively around her baby, and she leaned down and pressed a kiss to her sweet forehead.

If they didn't find a way to stop the wizards, Tesla would never reach adulthood.

Forest sighed, closed her eyes, and leaned her head against the back of the rocking chair. She pushed the chair into motion again with the slightest pressure of her heel against the floor and contemplated the biggest problem. No matter which way she considered it, Regia had no chance in a war against the wizards. There was no strategy, or weaponry, that could defeat them. They must be stopped before they could come in. Regia needed a wall that could hold back their force and keep them out.

It's not hopeless. It's not! She told herself forcefully.

Regia's best talents and minds were working tirelessly to solve the nasty equation. Her father, her mate, all of the masters of the Kata, Merhl, among many others. And now they had Journey. Journey had said many times that she didn't have an answer. But Forest believed when they found an answer, Journey would contribute a great deal, in the unique way only she could.

Her mind banged around and around on the problem. Nothing had changed. No new ideas came to her. She dozed off. Just a few moments of relaxation. Her breathing slowed, and the rocking chair stood still. It was short. Tesla roused and placed her tiny palm against Forest's neck, jolting her awake with a painful snap of electrical energy. Forest's muscles jerked in response to the pain, and Tesla began to cry.

She stood and paced the floor, trying to calm the baby. Her throat clenched, and her eyes stung as Tesla waved her tiny fists in the air, lightning snaking over her little fingers. Her soft arms trembled as she pushed her hands toward Forest's face and screamed. Her scream resounded of agony. Tears ran silently down Forest's cheeks. She would take the pain on herself, take everything that hurt her daughter into herself, if only she could.

She lowered herself to the floor, sitting cross-legged, laying Tesla in her lap. Forest took one deep breath, preparing for the pain, and pressed both of her daughter's hands against her chest, just above her breasts.

She clamped her mouth shut and closed her eyes tight. The magic in Tesla's hands burned hot as well as stung electrically. The power absorbed into Forest, and the baby quieted. A terrible buzzing filled her up and muffled her ears.

Forest jumped in alarm and opened her clenched eyes as she sensed someone next to her. Rahaxeris looked blurry as he laid his hand gently on her shoulder and then took the baby from her arms. Forest winced as Tesla's little hands pulled away, leaving burned marks behind, scorched black. It took a few seconds for the static in her ears to clear.

"What did you say?" she asked her father.

He frowned, and then turned his gaze to his granddaughter. He touched her hands, the red current absorbing into his long fingers. She stopped crying and gurgled happily at him.

"I asked why you were letting her touch your bare skin like that? I've warned you it could be dangerous."

Forest touched the burns on her chest gingerly. They would be gone in a while, a few hours at most. "I couldn't soothe her." Her voice was desolate. She looked at Rahaxeris smiling down at Tesla. "It's so unfair."

"What is?"

"You have the power to ease her pain. Syrus, too. I can't. Both of you get to play with her because she feels better with you. All she does is cry when I hold her."

He nodded, a sadness pulling around his eyes. "Stand up, Forest."

She sighed and stood.

"Here, take her."

Forest shook her head. "No. She's happy with you."

As if to confirm what her mother said, Tesla took that moment to blow a very wet raspberry at her grandfather.

"I think I'm just greedy with her. I never hand her back to you after I've pulled the pain from her hands."

Forest sighed and shook off her sadness. "You're entitled to be greedy... So, is there any news? Any new ideas?"

"Nothing I feel very optimistic about. I think it's time for me to go off world again. Journey has given me some useful information about some of the wizard's most powerful enemies. I'm thinking about going to them and throwing Regia on their mercy. To see if they will become our allies."

She chewed her bottom lip. "But we'd be dead weight to them, right? I mean, why would they protect us? Is there anything we have to offer they would want?"

"I'm not sure. That's why I need to go. I think they will at least give me the time to plead our case. It's worth a shot."

"The enemy of my enemy is my friend?" Forest offered him a small smile.

"That's my hope," he said seriously. Then he wrinkled his nose, and his voice went all goofy as he spoke to Tesla. "Yeassss, it is, pretty girl. Your grandpa is going to commune with scary people. Yes, he is. Yes, he is."

Forest snorted. Tesla giggled and blew another raspberry as she grabbed Rahaxeris' nose. Time slowed down and almost stopped as Forest looked at her father, holding her daughter. Her heart swelled and absorbed the moment. For so long, she'd lived thinking she'd never have these things. Or experience real love, family, and life. Life, in its invisible circles and its fleeting moments of joy. Gilded moments that sparkled. Life was pain, but the moments were there, collected and hidden inside her heart. Intangible and immortal memories that no one could take away from her.

"What do you think, Forest?"

She shrugged and shook her head. "I don't know. We have to keep moving until we find the answer. Does Merhl have any new ideas?"

"Too many. It's frustrating him. He's going with me off world."

"That's good. I feel better that you're not going alone. When are you planning to leave?"

He kissed Tesla on the forehead. "Tomorrow. I need to get back to Kyhael and prepare for my trip. But I couldn't leave without seeing my girls."

Forest came up beside him, placed her hand on his shoulder, and looked down at her baby. Tesla looked back at her and squawked out a funny noise.

"What do you see? She grows in odd spurts." Forest touched Tesla's cheek. "Will she grow out of this...this distortion?"

He frowned. "I wish I could tell you 'yes.' I don't think so. But I don't know for sure. She's so young. She has a lot to show us, yet. Her road will be hard. Of that I have no doubt. She'll have to learn to cope."

Forest turned her back as tears stung sharply in her eyes. "I want her to *thrive!* Not cope."

"I know, daughter. I know. Channel your anger into something useful."

"I don't know if I can," she admitted honestly. "I can't sleep. I cry so much at night. When it's dark, all my problems get bigger...overwhelming."

"You're not alone. Tesla is yours *and* Syrus'. Let him help you. And you have to help him through this as well."

Forest turned back to her father and narrowed her eyes. "Sage advice from a staunch bachelor."

He smiled.

"Don't worry about us. We're good. I swore I'd never pull away from Syrus again. I'm not about to break my word, or my heart like that." She rubbed her head and sighed. "I just feel so...brittle."

"You are. It won't last forever... You know, I'm going to do all I can for Tesla. You know that, don't you?"

Forest nodded. "Yes. I do."

"We'll learn more as she grows. It's too soon for me to know exactly what to do now. I'm not going to risk making a mistake with her." He kissed Tesla's forehead again and handed her back. "I need to go. Wish I didn't have to."

Tesla squeaked and waved her little fists in the air. He touched both of her hands, pulling out the power again. She smiled a toothless smile at her grandpa, her dimples coming out to play in her chubby cheeks. He gave Forest an awkward, one-sided, shoulder hug before leaving.

Forest watched him go from the window. "I love you, Dad," she whispered. "Come back safe."

She looked down at Tesla, who gazed at her expectantly.

"It's just you and me, baby. At least for a few more hours till your father comes home. What do you want to do?"

She set the baby on a blanket on the floor and placed a few toys around her. For a while, Tesla was happy. Forest sat on the floor and played with her. Her heart swelled at the peaceful time, knowing it would be short. She clung to every second greedily and let go of any thoughts of the encroaching danger. At this moment, while her daughter was free of her pain, she wasn't Hailemarris, she was just Mommy. It was wonderful for an entire hour...then it all went to hell again.

****

By sunset, Tesla was overtired and screaming in pain. Forest had swaddled her up, put her in her cradle, and closed the door to the nursery. She hated to do that. Hated it and hated herself, but there was nothing else for her to do. Tesla was dry and fed, and even though she cried, she was safe and would eventually cry herself to sleep.

Forest closed herself in her bedroom to try to block out the baby's cries. She lay down and put her fingers in her ears. But the spiritual connection between mother and child was stronger, and it didn't work. Tears streaming down her face and her heart pulling tight, she went back to the nursery. She sat on the floor next to the cradle and rocked it.

"Shhhh, sweetheart," she whispered. "Shhhhh…"

Tesla stopped screaming for a moment, just long enough for Forest to hope, then she started again. Forest's head pounded, and time seemed to fragment. She hummed and continued to rock the cradle.

Syrus appeared in the doorway. Forest looked up at him through blurry, bloodshot eyes. He didn't say anything at first. He came into the room and surveyed the scene for a moment. He reached down and took Forest by the hands, pulling her to her feet. She slumped against him. He gently stroked her hair back from her face and hugged her tightly before turning and picking Tesla up.

The baby was so worked up and exhausted that even when he held onto her hands and eased her pain back, she still didn't quiet.

Forest began to cry again, feeling helpless and guilty. "I can't…I just…can't." She stalked into the living room and sat down on the couch.

Syrus followed her. "Here." He held Tesla out to her.

Forest shook her head.

"She needs *you*," he insisted.

"No. She'll go to sleep for you. I'm drained…I've got nothing left, Syrus. I'm sorry."

He pressed. "We'll put her down together."

"Huh?"

He held the baby to her chest until her arms came up around their daughter. Forest sighed as Tesla continued to scream. Syrus sat down next to Forest and pulled her into his lap. She smiled at him as he held her in his arms and she held Tesla. His arms wrapped all the way around her and the baby. He moved slowly, and Forest relaxed against him. They rocked the baby together.

Forest fell head over heels in love with Syrus again. *I'm so lucky to have you. You're awesome. I don't know how I'd live without you.* Even though she didn't say the words aloud, he would catch her feelings through their connection.

Tesla quieted, yawned, and was out cold in a minute flat. For a while, they just stayed like that.

"She's deep now, Forest," Syrus whispered in her ear. "Go put her in her room, and we can have dinner."

Tesla didn't stir at all as Forest laid her back in her cradle. She kissed her forehead, and then her cheeks, before quietly closing the nursery door. Syrus came up behind her and placed his hands on her shoulders, rubbing them in deep circles.

"I'm not really hungry."

"That's fine. Dinner can wait," he said.

"I think I'm just going to go to bed. I'm so tired." She sighed and shook herself. "Sorry...I guess we should talk first." She turned around and faced him. "Rahaxeris came by, he said he's going to—"

He placed his index finger against her lips and smiled. "Shhh...I don't want to talk about that right now."

"You want to talk about Tesla." It wasn't a question.

"No... Look at me."

She did, questioningly at first. He cupped her face easily in his hands as she stared at him. His black pearl eyes bore down slowly on hers as she did as he asked and looked at him. Her heart did a little trip. She looked at him all the time. He was her life mate. But even after the amount of time they had been bound together, she still didn't find him commonplace. He was perfect, in every way. Kind, loving, fun, laid back, and so many other wonderful things. But he was also devastating to look at.

Every tension inside her sighed and let go. She reached up and ran her fingers through his shadowy black hair.

"I missed you today," she whispered. "I miss you whenever you aren't with me...I had such a bad day."

"I know. I felt it."

"I'm sorry. I wish you didn't have to feel what I do."

He looked down at her chest, where her skin was still discolored from the burns. His fingers ran lightly over the damaged skin, and his healing power gave her a little shock that buzzed more than hurt. He picked her up and held her tightly against his chest. "I'm glad you can't hide what you feel from me," he said quietly against her ear as he carried her through the house to their bedroom. "You're a better mother than you realize."

Tears built again behind her eyes. "I'm not...I just—"

"No more of this today. Nothing can be achieved by dwelling on the pain or the massive problems of the world, which no one has solved yet." His voice was soothing. "The day and its problems are over now. I know what you're feeling. And I know what you need. I'm going to do my best to wipe your mind clean of everything." He kissed her mouth, her eyes fluttering shut. "No more talking, unless you're screaming my name."

She snorted as he set her on the bed. "When do I ever do that? I'm not a screamer."

He knelt in front of her and took off her shoes. "You will be tonight."

She laughed lightly. "Not a good idea, babe. I'll wake the baby, then all the fun will be over real fast."

His face fell in disappointment. "Oh, right..." He closed his eyes, his expression going smooth and euphoric.

"Syrus?"

"I'm just imagining you screaming." He opened his eyes and smiled devilishly at her. "Okay, I'm good now. I just have to adjust my approach."

He eased her down slowly, all traces of teasing vanished. Intimacy was a regular part of life for them. They were used to each other. But that night he was different. *Every* kiss, *every* touch was about her. He healed her brittle and brokenness by forfeiting any thought of his own pleasure and gave everything to her. Life came back into her body under the touch of his deft hands, and her dried up heart flooded. His heart poured love into hers through their spiritual connection. She looked up at him as he loved her. So gorgeous. All man. All hers. Forever.

"Bite me," she whispered.

Amazing, tingly warmth spread through her body as he sank his fangs into her shoulder.

He broke her all the way down, and then built her back up again. His love gave her strength. Everything was fine. She could handle anything.

"I love you." Her voice came out barely audible before she crashed into sleep in his arms. Forest slept better that night than she ever had.

****

Journey went to the Wolf's Wood at the onset of night. The End of the Bridge she'd used set her down close enough to the Heart that she could see it in the distance. She approached slowly and with respect. Her bare feet grounded her to the power that ran in a constant current under the soil. She closed her eyes and exhaled, feeling the subtleties of the Heart's connections. She didn't have a name for it. It was like its own entity, like a consciousness, like a person, only not. The Heart was elusive...shy.

The crystal trees circling the flames chimed a disjointed tune, like a musician that was drunk, or exhausted. Sorrow and confusion filled every note.

Journey walked up to the crystal tree that was different. The one that was cloudy. The ghostly couple entwined inside still looked etched. They were frozen. She had no doubt they were real people, real souls trapped by malice, or perhaps their own free will—she couldn't tell. It was painful to look at them. They were a beautiful embodiment of heartbreak. Could she access their hearts? She had never tried to read the dead before. She hesitated. Perhaps it should wait. She gazed back on the flames. This was what she'd come here to learn about.

Journey walked into the circle. No heat came from the flame. She reached out and touched it with one fingertip. Like flowing water, a rush of energy ran over her skin where she made contact. It caressed her finger and probed up her hand, like a handshake, like a question. As if it asked, *who are you?*

Perhaps it did. She thought it best to answer just in case.

"My name is Journey," she whispered.

The music chiming in the crystal leaves changed, grew louder, and sounded like a woman crying. She pulled her hand back. A terrible sorrow settled through Journey, but it wasn't her sorrow. The Heart pushed it on her, like an intruder, shoving through a door. She struggled with it for a second, then she relaxed and opened herself up to it. She put her whole hand in the flames. *Show me. Make me understand.*

Journey choked as it rushed inside her. A surge of power swelled and threw her backward out of the circle. She landed on her back, her head hitting the ground, knocked unconscious.

"Journey...wake up."

She blinked and looked up at the stars winking through the canopy of trees. She breathed easily, feeling Redge's arm under her. She focused on him and smiled.

"I'm all right."

"What happened?"

"Just a little misunderstanding. The Heart and I got off on the wrong foot... It's no big deal. I'm not hurt."

She sat up and blinked a few more times, looking over at the flames. Excitement and determination coursed all through her. *We're not done.*

Redge backed away as she got to her feet and again approached the manifestation. This time she stayed outside the circle of crystal trees. Journey knelt down and placed her palms flat on the ground. "I'll come back later. We'll talk again."

CHAPTER TWO

Sabra lived in stone. It had always been like that. Born of the middle class, to a respected family, she and her brother and sister enjoyed the luxury of living in the mountain. Their family home was positioned on the coveted east face of the Lair. The most prized feature to their home was the terrace. Carved from the mountain itself, like a jutting lower jaw, the railing resembled a perfect set of teeth. That was how Sabra always thought of it. As a young girl, she'd realized how lucky she was in the unique features of her room especially. The stone of the mountain was typical grey and brown, but her room was carved through a unique white vein with tiny shimmering flecks that caught the light. The vein snaked down from the ceiling on one side, as thick as her hand.

The other special feature of her room was a small arched window that let in the morning sunlight and gave her a clear view of the main square on the ground below. She always knew what was happening because of this. She could hear the talk of the people clearly through her window.

Her parents didn't know the effect this would have on her in her formative years. If they had, they surely would have moved her to another room. As it was, Sabra grew up with her finger on the pulse of Werewolf society. And she formed strong opinions. Rock hard resolute ideas about her culture— what it was doing right, where it was going wrong—and detailed, realistic solutions about how they should evolve.

Sabra was a natural leader. It should have been easy for her to move into the role she longed for. The role she seemed destined to fulfill. There was just one problem. One nasty little detail that stood in her way.

She was female.

Wolf culture was nothing if not fiercely misogynistic.

She heard the shuffling of feet in the square, but she didn't look. Her heart threatened to start racing. She took a deep breath and forced her pulse to remain steady by sheer will. Today would determine her fate. She wouldn't submit to Tucker's matchmaking. Her brother meant well by trying to fulfill his duty to secure her with a good man, since their parents were dead. But she wasn't made to submit to a man. Any man.

So, despite that it was *frowned* upon, she would speak in the square this morning. She hadn't told anyone her plans. She would have told Sophie...Sophie, sweet baby sister, murdered by the insurgents.

The insurgents were no more. Their leader, Copernicus, was dead by the hand of the Hailemarris. Sabra burned to exact her revenge for Sophie, but she no longer had a target.

Except for *him*. The one she met that terrible night.

His face was chiseled deep in her consciousness. She didn't know his name, or even if he was still alive. But the blame for Sophie's murder fell on him. He'd said he hadn't killed her but openly admitted he did nothing to save her either.

Sabra held her breath for ten seconds. She counted the numbers slowly, looking at Sophie in her mind's eye. *I'm going to change things, baby sister. I promise.*

The sounds of more people coming to the square brought her back to the here and now. No matter what happened, she wouldn't cry. The night Sophie had died, Sabra cried more tears than she thought were physically possible. The next morning she'd sworn to herself she would never cry again. Not over anything, be it heartbreak or a stubbed toe. Her last tears were a sacred memorial to her sister. Sabra revoked the world's right to hurt her ever again.

Half of her was numb to fear. Just half.

She *was* going to change things. Someone had to. Her culture was backward and racist. And now was the time. The last war with the vampires had taken out most of their mature, established men. Her father being among them. There was no pack leader. The tournament was coming. The winner would be the new alpha...

And she would fight.

"Sabra? Can I come in?" Tucker asked from behind her door.

"Yeah." She turned away from the window.

He sauntered in, and she held back the insult to his appearance and demeanor that bubbled up her throat. For the last few weeks he'd started to mix with the wrong crowd, and he was trying to mimic them. She knew her sweet brother was still there, under the asshole mask he now wore.

"What do you want? I was about to go down to the square."

He frowned. "You don't need to go. You need to let go of your obsession about the pack's leadership... That's sort of what I wanted to talk to you about. It's time you settled down into your real role. I think I may have found you a mate."

Sabra ground her teeth together. This could go nuclear in two seconds flat. She clenched her fists, pouring everything she felt into her hands. She forced a smile.

"I told you, I'm not ready."

"That's not for you to decide," he said firmly, his cheeks coloring red with anger. "I'm trying to do right by you. I care who you are mated to. I'm doing my best to secure your future with a good man...and that's not easy when you have such a bad reputation."

"*What?!* Bad reputation?"

"Never mind."

"Oh, no. What bad reputation? If I have one, I certainly didn't know about it. You better tell me."

"You don't want to know."

"Maybe not. But I have a right to know," she demanded. "How can I defend myself when I don't know what I'm accused of?"

He crossed his arms over his chest. "Let's just say people know you fancy yourself an alpha. You're a shrew... The guys like to look at you, but then you open your mouth and prove yourself to be too much trouble. You're too wild. Any man willing to take you on is going to have to break you and make you submit. There are a few who would love to, let me tell you. But I don't want you mated to a violent sort who'd get off on beating you...and I don't want you with a weakling who would let you tug him around like a puppy and shame our family name...I love you." He took a deep breath. "I'm trying to do right by you," he said again. "You could try and make it a little easier on me."

So many words swirled in her mind. So many things she wanted to say. *It's not my destiny, brother.*

"I promise to *think* about what you've said. All right?"

"Good." His voice was clipped. He turned and headed back out of her room.

"Tucker?"

He looked back at her.

"Who is it?"

"Gahu."

Sabra didn't feel dread at the thought of being paired with Gahu. She didn't feel anything. "Are you negotiating with him? Have you struck a deal?"

"The deal is not sealed, yet. He wants you to settle into the idea first. He wants to spend some time with you."

Sabra groaned internally. "I'll think about it. But I can't say more than that."

He left her room. She looked back out the window. Arguing had already begun in the square. That was where she belonged. Anger surged through her. Tucker had put her on the auction block. Despite what her brother said, he wanted the status of selling her to whoever could pay the highest price. Damn their culture. Damn their traditions. She wasn't property. She *refused* to be property. And she'd give hell to any man who treated her as such, be it her brother or her mate. Screw men in general. She didn't need or want one.

She headed down to the square. Tucker was going to kill her for what she was about to do. So be it.

Her hands shook slightly as she moved into the hoard of people, pushing through to the front where she could be next to the boulder people stood on to give speeches. Silhon was standing on the rock at the moment, postulating and waving his arms in the air as he riled everyone up. He was one of the punks she wished Tucker didn't hang out with.

She listened closely to make sure she didn't miss anything she wanted to refute. It was a critical time for werewolves. The next leader would decide if they stayed steeped in tradition or if they'd move on to something...else. The young men saw it was their chance to take the reins because there were so few older men left. She might not have cared, except the loudest voices, the ones who wanted to become the leader, spoke of pushing their women down further. They also were touting the racism, hard. Wolves were superior and should remain aloof from the other races, blah, blah, blah.

"Now, more than ever, we must stick together and keep to ourselves. Regia is mixing all over the place in this new republic. I want nothing of it. It won't last. We all know it! We know the vampires and their love of ultimate power."

Most of the people around her raised their voices in agreement. Silhon continued.

"If we buy into this ruse of equality and mixing the Hailemarris is feeding us, we will die! It's a plot formed by the suckers!"

"The Hailemarris *is* for the people! All the people. Even us," a voice rang out from the crowd.

Everyone looked. Asher, one of the older generals, was the one who spoke.

Silhon hesitated, looking flustered. "But how can we trust her?" he plunged ahead. "She's not a vampire, but she may as well be one, seeing as she's mated to the Sanguine… And what of that?! A *woman* in a place of power with a mage at her side! She's the last person we should trust to have our best interests. And we all know who she really is. Forest, the smuggler, who used to hate vampires more than most of us. Or so she said."

Sabra took a deep breath, keeping her thoughts inside. It wasn't her time. Not just yet. She'd heard the gossip that Forest used to come to the Lair and had some dealings with Philippe. Sabra didn't know if this was true or not.

"We can't worry about the rest of Regia. We have to see to ourselves. The tournament will be on the first full moon of the Savage Solstice. And I will fight. I will be the next pack leader."

Some of the pack cheered for him. He absorbed the praise like a sponge. She could almost see his ego swelling beyond its already exaggerated size. He jumped down. Before anyone else could climb up on the rock, she pushed forward and vaulted onto it. An audible gasp went up from the crowd. Silhon turned and looked at her. He leapt back up on the rock and got in her face.

He pushed into her space until his face was an inch from hers. "What are you doing?" His voice was saturated with swagger.

"I'm going to speak."

He turned to the people and laughed as though they all shared a joke. "Sabra wants to speak." He faced her again, snarling. "I don't think so, bitch."

Both his hands slammed into her chest, knocking her off the rock. The air was knocked from her lungs as she hit the ground. Laughter rose up around her. She looked up at Silhon, laughing and pointing at her. All right. If that's how he wanted it. She took one breath and charged back up next to him. Her fist slammed into his nose, and he fell flat onto his back. His head snapped back against the ground, knocking him unconscious. Instant uproar and chaos ensued.

"I have earned my right to speak through force!" she shouted.

"Listen to me!"

The people quieted, and everyone looked at Samuel, the oldest male, and the most respected. Everyone was looking to him to guide them through this transitional time. No one else held the amount of authority.

He glared at Sabra, but then slowly nodded his head. "Let her speak."

She swallowed and balled her shaking hands as everyone turned their eyes back onto her. She looked over the tops of their heads, so she wouldn't accidentally make eye contact with Tucker. "We are at a crossroads. We have a vital role in Regia, but we have been hiding from it. It's not strength to hold only to our own, it is fear. We are a strong and proud people, as we should be. But how can we have pride in ourselves when we won't step up and help others who need us? Wolves have been close allies and friends with Shifters since the beginning of time. Our friends have been attacked and displaced by the insurgents, and what have we done to help them? Nothing!

"We were lucky Copernicus took no interest in us. But he saw fit to annihilate the shifter colony closest to us. Many of us had friends who died there. How have we honored the dead?"

She hesitated as she realized they were listening. She must not lose the thread of what she wanted to say. Her time was running short. She would be shut down soon for no other reason than she had a vagina.

"Things need to change! I will be our voice to the rest of the world, as the new leader...I will fight in the tournament."

Uproar again. This time was different than before. The half of her that still knew how to fear became awake. Very awake. She wouldn't have been heard, even if she shouted at the top of her lungs. Silhon had come to, and she found him invading her space again. His fist slammed into her jaw. The punch was weak and sloppy, but the force knocked her back. She didn't hit the ground like before. Instead, she was caught by a group of rough hands and restrained. Silhon's little punk gang had her, and they pulled her away from the crowd. Tucker wasn't there with them.

They were taking her away from the Lair and into the woods. No one seemed to notice, or if they did, they didn't care. She didn't scream. She didn't fight...yet. She wouldn't waste her strength struggling until she could do some damage with it. Silhon would be first. He'd use his lackeys to hold her, no doubt, while he beat her, or raped her. Maybe they all would take a turn on her. They'd be sorry.

"Hey!" A gruff, angry voice halted them.

Asher and Gahu approached behind them.

"Turn her loose!" Asher demanded.

"Get lost, old man," Silhon said. "We're going to teach this bitch a lesson about her place. She doesn't have any rights."

"Says who?" Asher demanded. "You're not the leader yet, boy. And until you are, you will not create laws that don't exist. There's nothing that says she can't challenge you in the tournament. Too bad you were flat on your back, taking a nap while she spoke. She's got more brains than you. I'd follow her any day over you."

Silhon spit on the ground. "It doesn't matter what you say. We're going to have a little private party here, and you're not invited. Don't worry, we won't kill her. Now get lost."

Gahu stepped forward. "I'm in negotiations with Tucker for Sabra. She's basically my betrothed. She overstepped today, but her discipline is mine to administer. Let her go."

Silhon sneered at Gahu, and then laughed derisively. He signaled for his gang to let go of her. She didn't run like a damsel in distress. She walked slowly past Silhon. "I'm going to kill you in the tournament. Maybe I'll take a page from Philippe's book and turn your pelt into a cloak." She smiled. "Or perhaps a nice hat and a pair of gloves. I've seen you in wolf form. Your pelt is so pretty."

Color rose up his face, and he bared his teeth.

"Sabra!" Gahu yelled. "That's enough! Come here."

She winked at Silhon and walked over to Gahu. He wrapped his arm around her shoulders and drew her away possessively.

"Watch your step." Asher warned the punks before turning and following Gahu.

She waited until they were out of earshot of her would-be abusers.

"Thank you," she said, looking up at Gahu's profile.

He didn't stop walking, and he didn't look at her. He just pulled her along until they came to the main entrance of the Lair. Where Asher stopped following.

"Don't disgrace yourself, Gahu, by treating her like any other man might," Asher warned.

Gahu shook his hand but ignored the advice. "Thanks for your help."

He nodded curtly. "I think we're going to have to look out for her till the tournament. Silhon will continue to try and take her out where no one can see what he does."

"She won't be fighting in the tournament," Gahu said gruffly.

Before she could say anything, Asher smiled at her. "I bet she does." He turned and walked away. "I'm with you, Sabra," he said over his shoulder. "You've got my support."

Gahu pulled her down a hallway and pushed her up against the wall. "What were you thinking? You know Silhon and his gang are trouble. You publicly shamed him. What did you think was going to happen?"

"What did *you* think was going to happen?" she demanded. "You might be sniffing the air around me, making a deal with my brother, but you don't know me at all. I wouldn't have been able to take all of them out by myself, but I could have gotten damn near close. I'm a superior fighter. Most of those bastards are lazy and couldn't land a blow to me even trying their hardest."

"They had your arms, and you were outnumbered six to one... Stop bragging."

She crossed her arms and scowled at him. He wasn't any more than an acquaintance, but he didn't seem like a bad sort. Quite a bit older than her, but still in his prime. He was rough around the edges and worn from the war. Everything about him was brown. Rich brown eyes, reddish brown hair, and dark tanned skin. He was a skilled soldier, and he'd survived the war when so many others hadn't. Being his might not be so bad. If it weren't for the fact that was exactly the way he would treat her, as *his*.

"So, what was that you said? My *discipline* was yours to administer?"

He narrowed his eyes. "That's right." His fingers dug roughly into her shoulders as his mouth came down on hers. In that moment, she hated him.

"Very sweet, under the sour surface," he said, licking his lips.

She gave him the most malevolent glare she could muster. "Regrettably, I cannot return the compliment."

Anger flashed in his eyes, and his nostrils flared. His fingers dug a little deeper into her shoulders, then he released her and took a step back. The fire in his eyes eased back, and then to her surprise, he laughed.

"I'm sorry. I shouldn't have been forceful with you... Take some time to get to know me, Sabra. I think you'll find we can get along."

She pursed her lips. "Why do you want me at all? Apparently, I have a bad reputation."

"I don't care about that. You've earned your reputation though. It's not unjust, what is said of you."

"You didn't answer my question."

He snorted and ran his hand through his hair. "I have my reasons. Most of them are not very sexy. Status, stability, strength, family, and so on..." He looked at her more intently. His gaze raking her from her toes and back up to her face. "And then there's that—" his voice went quiet "—*animalistic* reason."

She waited to feel something at his proclamation of desire. He didn't repulse her. He was attractive. There was just...nothing. Sure, it stroked her ego to know he wanted her, but it seemed that was all. He reached and took her hand. She gave it.

"Can we try that again?" he asked.

She hesitated, and then nodded, allowing him to pull her against his chest and kiss her mouth. It was nice, but there was no fire. At least not for her.

"Can I see you tonight?"

She wanted to be alone. He was suffocating. She needed to think about what had happened and what she'd done. Tucker was going to kill her. She'd have to deal with him. Maybe that was her out with Gahu, for now.

"I'm sure Tucker is going to be furious with me for speaking in the square. I doubt he'll let me out tonight. Sorry."

He looked thoughtful. "I'll talk to him."

She barely kept her eyes from rolling. "Great. I've got to go now."

Before she could leave, he kissed her again. She walked away thinking about his kiss. Nope. Still nothing.

She walked up the winding rock stairs to her family's mid-level home. The place was empty, or so she thought. She moved through the main living space to her room. As soon as she came through the door, Tucker was there. He backhanded her.

She looked up at him from the floor and licked the blood on her mouth. Her face burned and ached, and her ears hummed. He'd never hit her that hard before.

"Have you lost your mind?!" he shouted. "Not only do you speak publicly, you declare that you're going to fight in the tournament! No woman has ever been the pack leader. Ever! I can't even...You have no clue the damage you've done to yourself...to me! There's no way I'm going to find you a mate now."

"Oh really?" she challenged. "Because Gahu was just kissing these lips you've just bloodied. He wants to see me tonight. He's more interested than ever. He's not the same level of sexist you are."

Tucker looked shocked. "He's still interested? Well...good. Maybe I can push the two of you together faster, and then he'll keep you busy and away from trouble...or if not, at least you'll be his problem and not mine."

"I'm never going to change, Tucker. This is who I am. Your problem or not. The pack is mine to lead. I feel it in my bones. It's my destiny. You better settle with the idea."

He scoffed at her and shook his head.

"Just because I'm a woman doesn't mean I don't know how to lead."

He reached down and offered his hand. She took it, and he pulled her to her feet. He looked at her bleeding mouth, and remorse filled his eyes.

"Even if it were true, you can't win the tournament. You were too young to witness the last one, when Philippe took over. It's not just a fight... It's a fight to the death. Only one victor. The one who survives."

"I know!" She didn't know, but she covered it with bluster.

"You have to withdraw your name."

"No! I put my name in. Everyone heard me. I...I'm not backing out."

"Then you will have to kill, or you will die."

Cold dread pooled in her stomach. What had she gotten herself into?

CHAPTER THREE

Asher stood by the river and looked up at the moon, smoking his pipe. He thought about shifting into his wolf form and experiencing the moon as only a wolf can. He thought about the events of the day and the pack. It was hard for him to wrap his brain around where they were and where they had come from. He'd seen Philippe rise to power, lead them in a march of insanity through a humiliating war, and then die by the hand of a female vampire.

Women, he mused, thinking of Sabra.

She was different. But she was right. He agreed with everything she'd said, not that she'd had the time to say that much. Still. He was going to look out for her and make sure she had every opportunity to speak. He had a feeling Gahu wasn't going to help her rise to power. He might not hurt her much, but he wanted her in submission as his mate. Asher planned to help her train to fight in the tournament, if she'd let him. She had a chance. She wasn't a slip of a girl. She was muscled and taller than most females. She certainly had guts.

She'd need them.

In truth, he'd considered adding his name to the list of those fighting, but now... He had a feeling about Sabra. He was old, and it was time for the young to step up and lead the next generation. The young women needed a good role model like Sabra. They deserved to have a choice and opportunity.

He took a long drag from the pipe, about to toss it down and shift when his ears pricked. He turned around, feeling them approaching before he could see or smell them. Punks...out for blood. That was just fine with him. He'd show them what experience, matured through violence, could do.

****

Tucker took off for a while and then returned right before dinner as the moon climbed up the sky.

"Well you're the talk of the pack," he said easily when he came home.

Sabra detected his displeasure under the surface. "Oh? What is—"

"I don't want to discuss it right now. My head hurts. Gahu will be coming by in a while to see you. I recommend you make yourself presentable."

"Presentable?"

"Yeah, fix your hair, wear something nice for him, girl stuff that makes guys crazy."

Sabra snorted. "Fat chance."

He scowled and heaved a sigh. "Hopefully, I can get you mated before he wises up and walks."

She ate dinner quickly, and then shut herself in her room. She looked down at her shirt. Small spots of blood dotted the fabric. She took it off and put on another one, not caring much how it looked. She wouldn't do more than that. She sat on her bed, pulled her knees up to her chest, and looked out her window at the moon. Weird, crazy day. She'd made her political ambitions known to the pack, and now she was sitting around waiting to have... a date? Ugh.

Was there a place, deep inside her, that wanted Gahu? Something natural, instinct perhaps, that would kick in and delight in submission to him? Every fiber of her being scratched and screamed at the thought. Submit? Guess not.

She heard the knock on the front door and thought about jumping out the window and running away. She wouldn't greet him at the door or act like she was anxious to see him. Because that's what it would be: acting. She heard Tucker let him in. The deep tones of their voices drifted under her door as they talked. She braced herself as a knock came to her door. She stood and answered.

Tucker stood scowling at her. "Didn't you hear him come in?" His voice was hushed. "Get out there and spend some time with him. And for goodness sake, be nice. You're lucky he's here."

"What am I supposed to do? Does he want to take me somewhere?"

"I don't know... Do whatever he wants."

Sabra gaped. "You're chaperoning me, right?"

"I don't see the need. If he still likes you after tonight, your mating will be set in a fortnight."

She narrowed her eyes. "And if he pushes the boundaries? Am I to just do *whatever* he wants?"

Tucker looked away so she wouldn't see the guilt in his eyes. She saw it anyway, and her hands fisted, aching to pummel him.

"Did you tell him to push me too far? To ruin my reputation beyond what it already is? So I have no way of getting out of it? I can see the shame all over you, Tucker! I'm right, aren't I?"

"Only half way," he shot back, grabbing her wrist painfully. "Now get out there and act like you think he's wonderful, even if you can't stand him."

"I will not!"

His fingernails dug into her skin, drawing blood. "I've had enough of you, Sabra. If you don't do as I say, I swear, I will hand you over to Silhon. One night with the boys, and you'll never be able to lift your head again."

She regarded him thoroughly and pulled her wrist free. "Look at me," she said quietly.

He did, his anger held still for a moment.

"What happened to my brother? I feel like I don't know you at all...I'll do what you want...for now. I'll spend time with Gahu, and I won't ruin your deal with him. But I won't let either of you shame me."

She brushed past him and gave Gahu her most charming smile. It almost felt real. She preferred his society over her brother's. He seemed like the lesser evil, at least for the moment.

He raised her hand to his lips and kissed it. "It's nice to see you. Would you care to go for a walk? The moon is wonderfully bright. I'd like to run with you as a wolf."

Sabra took a deep breath and tried to relax. What he asked for felt very intimate. She wasn't ready to shift in front of him. And if anyone knew they had run together, alone as wolves, the talk would be vicious. Instinct ran too strong, and reason was almost silent when in wolf form. She was sure he'd thought of this, too.

"That makes me a little uncomfortable. I'd like to wait for that, please... Perhaps we could enjoy the moon right here, on our terrace? That way Tucker can still chaperone."

He kissed her hand again, looking pleased. "Sure. That sounds nice...more appropriate. I'm sorry if my suggestion was too forward."

Damn good answer, she thought.

He held her hand as they walked out onto the terrace. The roughness and strength of his hand was appealing. At least he wasn't a wuss. She was trying to stay positive.

The moon was indeed bright. She tilted her head back and took a deep breath. The pale, aquamarine light of the moon reached down inside her and called to the beast there.

"You're beautiful, Sabra."

Her attention jumped onto him and her unguarded moment, enjoying the moonlight, now embarrassed her. She looked down. "Thank you."

"I'm not sure how to go about this...I feel foolish."

"You're not sure how to go about what?"

"Getting to know you. I'm afraid you're going to reject me...I think that's part of the appeal. The chase." He offered her a half smile. He really was quite handsome. Why didn't she like him more? Maybe she would in time.

Stupid wolf culture. Arranged mating worked out for the men. She should be grateful to be paired with a good guy, but there was more to life. Few found love through sheer luck. And the very rare werewolf found a destined life mate. That's what she wanted. She knew she was different, special. She wanted to know love. She'd be good at it.

The moon called harder. Maybe she could have what she was looking for with Gahu. Perhaps she should run with him. Would that feel different than this? More?

"What are you thinking about?" he asked.

"The future."

"That's good. I've been thinking about our future as well. Where we'll live, if you don't care for my apartments. They are smaller than this, but they are also higher up. There's enough room for our first few children...I think that—"

"Whoa! Just stop!"

"What?"

"I...too fast, Gahu. I said I was thinking about *the* future not *our* future."

He frowned and looked away from her. "How is it too fast when we'll be mated soon?"

"Look, I'm not saying no to you, but it can't be that fast. I have to focus on the tournament first. I'll never win, if I don't put it first."

He placed his hands on her shoulders and captured her gaze. "I like that you're strong. But you have to give this up. You'll die in the tournament."

"How do you know?"

"You cannot be pack leader," he said firmly.

"Because I'm a woman, right?"

"Yes. That's right. You're a woman, get over it."

She pulled away from him. "I'd hoped you'd be different."

"I am different. But I can't have you do this."

"Why?" she demanded louder than she'd meant to.

"Because I plan to fight as well. I can't fight against you. You're mine. You fighting is asking me to kill you, or watch someone else kill you."

"I put my name in first! I'm going to be leader. It's my destiny."

"No, Sabra." He pulled her against him and kissed her roughly. "I'm your destiny."

She had two choices: beat his brains in or close herself down. She thought of Tucker's threat to hand her over to Silhon. She turned away from him, braced her hands on the terrace railing, and sighed.

"I'm tired. I think I'll go to bed."

He caught her hand as she tried to walk back into the house. "Hey, are we all right?"

"Sure," she said flatly. "*We* are just fine. Why don't you and Tucker hammer out the details of our mating?"

He raised his eyebrows and smiled. "All right. Here, before you go..."

He pulled a carved wooden cuff bracelet out of his pocket and slipped it around her wrist. She sighed again and forced a smile. What had she done? Was her life over? Had she just forfeited it?

He kissed her again. She allowed it passively, and then went back inside and shut herself in her room. She sat on the edge of her bed. So Gahu was going to fight in the tournament. That wouldn't stop her. Would it?

She held her wrist up and looked at the bracelet. A tirade of curses crashed inside her mind like a massive wave hitting the sand. Had she been beaten already? Crushed. Subdued. Branded. How many rules could she break and bend before they bent and broke her? Were her aspirations worth her life?

She took the bracelet off and set it down so she didn't give in to temptation and break it into splinters. Their voices drifted in under the door again. This time, she crept to the door and pressed her ear against it.

"She's agreed, Tucker. I feel secure in proceeding. Let's get this done. I want her. I don't want to wait very long. She needs to be conquered before the tournament. I feel certain she will calm down and become what I want her to be. And if I become pack leader, she will be happy in her role beside me. She'll feel like she has some influence. And she will have *a little*."

"Good. Are you still comfortable with the price?" Tucker asked.

"I am."

"Then we'll spread the happy news tomorrow. That should calm the gossip down a bit. Silhon will let go of his vendetta against her, I think."

"Perhaps. Although I'm sure he'll be angered at my joining the fight."

"Are you wanting a private or public affair? It's been a while since anyone had a party for a mating," Tucker said.

"A party would be good. A few days before the tournament would put the pack in a good mood. Sabra will need something special to wear. I want every male to envy me that day. Her beauty must be displayed."

It felt like an inferno jumped to life inside her head. She couldn't listen anymore. She cracked her door and peeked out. They both had their backs to her. Perfect. She silently crept out of her room and made it back onto the terrace without them noticing. She vaulted over the railing. The wind rushed around her as she fell. The ground jostled her ankles painfully as she landed in the deserted public square.

She straightened and looked around. Lights glowed from the small wood homes in the Lair's suburbs. She charged off in a beeline, heading to the wilds. Never had she needed to be alone so badly, just to run.

****

Shreve sat on the ground, his back against a tree, quietly enjoying the night. He was close to the Wolf's Wood. The Lair just beyond. He'd determined to walk and not use any of his abilities, to move from place to place, instantly, through portals, because he suspected doing so would wind his time down faster. He didn't know this for sure; he just didn't want to risk it. Every moment was precious.

He gazed at the black outline of the Lair. Something held him back from beginning his dive into wolf society. Doubt that he could assimilate into their culture without drawing serious attention was in the front of his mind. They were a pack, all interconnected. They kept to themselves. He didn't think he could escape notice and just live in the background.

He still wanted to try, but the longer he thought about it, the less likely he was to do it. What did it matter anyway? He'd be dead soon. Why did he even want to try to live as wolf?

He leaned his head back and closed his eyes. Something about this night felt special. Would it be his last? Was that why he felt so alive?

The faint sound of running in the distance woke him to the moment. He opened his eyes and honed his hearing...

Oh, that is lovely.

He didn't move, and he couldn't see anyone yet, but he could hear her heart thundering, and her lungs pumping. She was very fast. Then, he saw her. She moved through the thick of trees as if they weren't there at all. The moonlight slid over her, lighting her up like a shimmering blade, cutting through the darkness.

He stood but didn't follow... yet. She turned and now ran flat out in front of him, away from him. He watched her back, her long hair flew out beautifully behind her. She'd be gone soon. Too far away for him to see. He thought about tailing her, and then decided against it. Why should he? She was running hard from something, or someone. Perhaps he would follow far behind, just to be sure a monster didn't stalk her.

Just as she was almost out of sight, she stopped short. He crept closer. She threw her head back and screamed. Three times, she emptied her lungs and then refilled them and screamed. He understood the utterance. She wasn't in terror. Her scream was that of rage and frustration. He pulled his elf DNA forward and went invisible.

She paced back and forth a few times. Her aura lit up around her. Shreve moved toward her like a moth to a flame. So much life radiated from her; he wanted to absorb some of it. It was angry life, caged, and struggling to break free.

He stopped before getting too close. He just wanted to watch her for a moment, not alert her to his presence. Something about her seemed familiar. He should just walk away and leave her to whatever it was she was going through. It probably wasn't right for him to watch her like this. He tried to consider the mysteries of right and wrong again. What did his gut tell him? Was he doing wrong by standing there, watching her when she thought she was alone?

Yes. He concluded it was wrong.

He took one silent step backward and then stopped dead. She took her shirt off and dropped it on the ground. Her pants followed. She looked up at the moon, totally naked. Her hair hung halfway down her bare back. Shreve couldn't make himself move. His base, male desires wanted her to turn around and face him so he could see the rest of her.

She sighed and ran her fingers through her honey colored hair. Then, her body began to change. She shifted into a wolf. The moon glistened in her fur just as it had in her hair. She had no spots or markings at all except a black ring on the tip of her tail. She turned on him, and he felt like he'd been punched in the gut. He knew those deep purple eyes.

Sabra.

The young woman he'd met only once, over her sister's dead body.

She sniffed the air. He couldn't hide from her now. Her ears flattened on her head, and a low growl rumbled in her throat. He didn't think. He just acted.

****

There was someone there. She couldn't see him. He was close—she could smell him. What was that scent? Did she know it? There was something off to his smell, almost *unnatural*, yet alluring.

Screw it. Whoever he was and whatever he wanted, he wasn't attacking her. She'd come here to run, and now she would. The moon filled her wolf body, refreshed and centered her. Her muscles ached to move.

She was on the verge of darting away when his eyes appeared in the dark. A wolf came toward her, fur blacker than midnight, eyes green like emeralds. A vibrant trauma flowed through her veins and went straight to her heart. His aura reached out to hers and grabbed hold. She reached back. The subtle channels of communication that only wolves could share opened between them. In wolf form, there was no way to lie or hide what you felt. Whoever this man was, she was connected to him. Drawn in. Taken over. Consumed by chemistry.

This was why she hadn't wanted to run with Gahu. The most basic nature, male and female, took over. But this was different. This was beyond, and again, unnatural.

How could there be a werewolf she didn't know? But she *didn't* know him.

She darted away, running flat out as fast as she could. He followed as she knew he would. It became a race. They ran neck and neck. She prided herself on being very fast, but he kept pace with her effortlessly. Had she wandered into a dream? Who was he? She'd never seen a more beautiful wolf in her life. Wolves were beautiful, all of them. But him...this black wolf was exquisite and otherworldly. Would he be as beautiful as a man? She desperately wanted to know.

Communication was in the psyche, beyond words. She didn't get much from him just a strangled kind of joy, somewhat fearful. He wanted her, she felt that, but he kept his distance. Content to just run beside her, just to be near her.

A powerful pull began inside her, as if she were tethered to him. He didn't behave as any other wolf would. He held instinct in check, or it was something else, like a confusion inside him as to how to treat her. She was thrown by that. He didn't attempt to establish dominance. Why? She didn't question his desire. He couldn't hide it from her. Just as he felt her attraction to him.

Sabra stopped running and drank from the river. He waited beside her. Teasingly, she slapped him on the snout with her tail, to see what he would do. He moved forward and caught her tail in his teeth. Oh, goodness, she was in trouble, in the best way.

He released her and lowered his head to just under her chin. A surge of remorse came from him, and he sank further down in a show of submission. She was confused. He was apologizing. For what? She pushed at him, mentally. Questioning him.

He jumped away and ran. She followed, only to have him turn on her. He growled a warning. She held still, more confused than ever. Their time together was over. He was leaving. He turned and disappeared into the night.

Sabra waited, disappointed and mystified. She would find out who he was. They were connected, somehow. She was sure she would see him again...well, she hoped. If she saw him in his man form, would she know it was him?

She ran home in wolf form, her mind spinning, forgetting her clothes altogether. Something profound had changed inside her. The black wolf had given her a new measure of strength. She would hold fast to her desires for her future. Even when others tried to break her hands, she would hold on.

****

Shreve followed Sabra at a great distance after shifting back into his normal state. His heart trembled. What had happened? What had he done? And why? He didn't know wolves shared a level of mental connection like that. Had he known, he definitely wouldn't have taken a wolf form next to her. Too late now. The experience rocked him to the foundation of his soul. It was honest, intimate, and carnal. It was terrifying that she could see him that deeply, and he could look that far into her in return. Absolutely terrifying.

And he wanted it again.

He went back to the place he'd been resting before she broke into his peace and shattered it. She'd left her clothes. Unable to help himself, he picked them up and buried his nose in her shirt before putting the garments in his bag with his own.

What are you doing? In all the world, in all the worlds that exist, she's the last woman that could be for you. Once she knows who you are...she will blame you for her sister's death, and rightly so. Once she knows, this misguided dream will end. He argued with himself. *She doesn't have to know.*

CHAPTER FOUR

Banging on the front door woke Sabra before the morning's light. Her sleep had been restless and filled with dreams of the black wolf. She groaned and rolled over on her bed, listening to see if Tucker would get up and get the door. The banging continued, became louder. Huffing out a breath, she got up and stalked through the house to the front door. It better not be Gahu.

To her surprise, it was Asher. He looked rumpled and had a black eye. She blinked at him for a moment.

"Come on. Get dressed, girl. It's time to start your tournament training."

"What?"

"You need help, if you're going to win the tournament. Silhon and his puppy pals attacked me last night. I gave them a through thrashing. They meant to intimidate me for standing up for you. The thing is, I paid close attention as I taught them a lesson. I know how they fight and the challenges you'll face with them. If you want to have a prayer of surviving, you better come with me."

Indecision wormed its way through her belly. "My brother and Gahu are trying to convince me I don't stand a chance. I think maybe they're right. Maybe I am crazy and should just pull my name out. They're both on the verge of *forbidding* me anyway."

"I wouldn't think such a trivial thing would thwart you. The decision is ultimately yours. They *technically* can't stop you, not according to the laws, probably because no one ever thought about the possibility... Anyway, will you at least give me today? Let's see what you can do. I swear, by the end of the day, I will give my honest opinion if you have a chance of winning or not. I will tell you the whole, brutal truth."

She bit down on her bottom lip as she mulled it over. Excitement began building in her at the thought of training.

"Why do you want to help me? I mean, I appreciate your support, but really, why?"

"Well, ultimately, I want to see you win so you can make things better for the women. We've been so closed off and well, you know. I think the pack needs a mother, not another vicious male."

"Mother?" Sabra frowned.

He smiled. "I know you're not an *actual* mother yet. But you can still be a mother to your people."

"Interesting."

"So are you coming with me or not?" he demanded.

"I'll be ready in a minute."

Sabra followed Asher. He led her away from the Lair, all the way to the dead area that used to be the shifter colony. She stopped short on the edge, not wanting to step foot on the still blackened ground. There were no remains of the shifters who died there, but there were still the charred skeletons of their homes.

Asher turned and looked at her when she stopped walking.

"Find your spine, girl," he ordered roughly. "This is the best place for you to train because no one wants to come here. You will have privacy." When she didn't move, he pushed. "You spoke of honoring those who died here. Do you think Silhon will do a damn thing for the shifters if he wins?"

Sabra shook her head slowly. "No."

She took a deep breath and stepped onto the blackened ground.

"Good," he said. "Don't shut it out. Look at it. Think of them. Remember them. Let their blood convict you. Fight for them as well as the pack."

She nodded. "Yes...I will."

"Okay, first thing. Do you know the rules of the tournament?"

"No," she admitted. "Except that it is a fight to the death. I only just learned that. I didn't know when I announced that I would be fighting."

He smiled approvingly. "And you're still here. You haven't withdrawn. So, yes, in order to advance in the tournament, you have to kill your opponents. That is the way it has always been done. You are allowed two weapons. Usually contenders will have a large weapon and then a smaller fall back, like a knife. This isn't really fair, because if you favor the sword, that doesn't mean your opponent has to use a sword as well. You might face a bow and arrow, or a mace. I didn't know what you might favor, so I put a selection of weapons here last night, for you to try... Have you done much weapons training?"

"No. Not much. A little with the staff," she admitted.

"The staff is good choice, because it is out of style. Those puppies you'll be facing will choose their weapons for flash."

"Gahu is fighting, too," she cut in.

"Hmm... That's not good. Are you prepared to kill him? Do you have feelings?"

"I don't know. I don't feel much, but I don't want to face off with him either."

"You should try to convince him to pull his name out. The two of you against each other is no good any way you slice it. He's a strong fighter, but I don't think he'd be able to force himself to hurt you. His feelings are probably stronger than yours. Even if he doesn't love you, you're his woman, so his instinct is to protect you..." He rubbed the stubble on his chin. "This is no good at all."

"Let's get started. I can think about this later."

"All right."

Asher gathered an armload of weapons from inside one of the ruined homes and laid them out for her. She looked down the row, thinking strategically, or trying to. Short swords, a broad sword, a mace, a staff, a crossbow, a regular bow, a club, various knives, and then...an old worn leather whip.

Sabra picked it up, a rush going through her as she ran her fingers over the braided coil. She'd never held a whip before, or even seen anyone use one. She gripped the handle, the thong falling loose next to her feet. She looked over at Asher.

He smiled. "Interesting choice. I can see you're already quite taken with it. It's honestly not a great option because it's very difficult to land a serious blow with a whip. Painful, and loud, sure, and it has a terror element that exceeds its capabilities, but—"

"But you said I can have two weapons. This adds intimidation and surprise, right? Who will expect me to show up in the ring, brandishing a whip?"

He smirked. "Okay. You might be right. I'll teach you. But you better pick a more deadly weapon for your second choice."

"I'll use a sword as my second."

She moved her wrist side to side, the end of the whip moving like a snake. She experimented, rolling her wrist, then carefully at first, she brought her arm over her head and swung out in a long arch across her body. She watched the reaction, knowing exactly where and how the whip would move and land before it did. She easily understood the physics of it. Something about it clicked with her. She had an innate, instant and intimate connection with the weapon. It was an extension of her.

Asher smiled. "Nice," he said appreciatively. "Now bring it up and let it fall behind you, keeping your hand level with your temple." He walked over, moving her elbow. "Always pause. Make sure the whip has touched the ground, or you might take your ear off. Now bring your arm straight down, easily. You don't need force on the down swing. Put more force into the upswing."

She nodded, and he backed away. She let her arm fall, so she could experience the full motion from the beginning, without his maneuvering her position. Up and over it went. The second she felt it touch the ground, she brought her arm down. The whip came back over and cracked.

"HA!" she exclaimed.

"Very good. That's a basic crack, useful for intimidation."

Excited, she cracked it three times in a row, already imagining how she could move it better, crack it louder, or in a more stylized way. She thought about how she could make it strike out at a target and split it open. Without asking permission to try, she took a step forward, turning in a graceful circle, bringing her arm up, mid turn, rolling her wrist, and snapping it. The whip rolled through the air, and cut through the charred wood beam of the closest roof.

Elated she looked to Asher. His eyes were wide. He blew out a breath. "I don't know if that was a display of natural talent, or just dumb luck... Do you know what you just did? Could you do it again?"

"Easy. I just imagined it before I did it."

He crossed his arms. "All right, showoff. Show me again, and I'll believe you."

She looked back at the remains of the burned house and picked a roof beam on the other side of the house. She felt her heart accelerate in excitement. Again she stepped forward and spun in a circle, bringing her arm up and rolling her wrist, but she missed her target. The whip struck six inches lower than she intended. The end hit the stone of the wall instead. Crumbled mortar and dust flew into the air off the wall. She swore loudly, disappointed.

"Don't let that get you down," Asher coached. "You were close... So perhaps you're a mix of natural talent and luck. Still damn impressive."

She sighed.

"Come on. You'll have plenty of time to practice. Now put that down. Let's see how much strength you've got hand to hand."

She placed the whip on the ground next to the other weapons. "Wait. Can I fight in beast form? Is that against the rules?"

"It's not against the rules, but most choose not to because it's damn near impossible to handle weapons when your hands are stretched like that. The deadly strength we have in beast form is all well and good against the other races, but it's fairly even when we fight each

45

other. Plus, your opponent isn't going to give you the few seconds it takes to shift. As soon as you begin the shift, it'll be over."

He rushed at her then. She stepped out of the way. He turned and came at her again. This time she turned her torso and slammed into him with her shoulder. He grunted as she elbowed him in the solar plexus. He grabbed her by both arms and swept her feet out from under her. She landed hard on the ground. She made to get up, but he held her down.

"This isn't a friendly game, Sabra. Give me everything you've got. No rules now. Any hits are legal. Show me how you would kill me."

She kneed him in the groin. His face blanched, but he didn't let go. She rolled to her stomach then brought her head up fast enough to crack him in the face. He backed off then, swearing. She launched at him, getting her arm in a choke around his neck. He fell backward, slamming her between his body and the ground, winding her and breaking one of her ribs.

Sabra croaked a gasp and looked up at him from the ground. She moaned and held her hands up in surrender. He sighed and reached down to help her up. She kicked out, just as he had, knocking his feet out from under him and jumping onto his chest. She slammed her fist as best she could into his face before grabbing him by the throat and choking him.

He reached up with one hand and tapped her twice on the shoulder. She let go and darted away in case it was a ruse. Her broken rib ground together. She clenched her teeth against the pain, determined to ignore it.

He sat up, coughing loudly. "Good. Very good," he rasped. "You tricked me. I like that. You may need to use deception in the tournament as well. Play the weak woman card."

He got to his feet. She still didn't drop her defensive stance. He smiled, wiping dirt from his backside. "Easy now. I'm not going to spring on you again. Not without warning first, at least not today."

She relaxed and hissed as her broken bone moved. "You broke my rib."

"You crushed my larynx," he countered.

"So, how did I do? You promised brutal truth."

"Better than I expected. With a bit more skill, you should fair just fine hand-to-hand. Your opponents aren't going to expect your strength or viciousness. You move fast. That being said, you still won't have the same level of brute strength because you're female. Don't jump down my throat for that, it's a fact of life. Just as you aren't disadvantaged by having your genitals as an easy target. Dirty move, by the way."

"Sorry," she said lightly.

"No you're not, nor should you be. Any chance you get to crush someone's nuts in the tournament, you better take it. Hear me?"

She nodded. "So what now?"

He looked up at the sky. "You better go home before someone notices you're missing. I want you to build up your body. Strength training every day. Get enough sleep at night. Focus on your health. Don't tell anyone about what we're doing and where we are. We've got three months to get you ready. I'll expect you back here two hours before dawn tomorrow. Got it?"

"Yes...Asher?"

"What?"

"Thank you."

He waved her thanks away dismissively. She turned to leave but stopped next to the row of weapons on the ground. She picked up the whip and glanced back at him.

He scowled and shook his head. "Leave it here. You don't want to risk losing the element of surprise if someone sees you with it."

Ruefully, she set it back down. "You're right."

Sabra walked slowly back home, trying to not move her upper body much, so as not to grind the rib anymore. She couldn't go totally unnoticed as she came into the main entrance of the Lair. Those standing guard didn't harass her or talk to her at all as she passed.

Tucker was still asleep when she slunk into the house. She breathed a sigh of relief and crept to her room. Her side stabbed terribly every time she breathed. She lay down on her bed and tried to relax, but she was buzzing. She was physically tired, not from fighting, but from lack of sleep. She closed her eyes and imagined the black wolf again. He had prevented her from sleeping most of the night. Her body was still humming after she came home from running with him, but then he ran through her dreams, the moonlight on his shadowy pelt. His emerald eyes on her. *I see you...I know you*...a deep voice whispered in her dreams.

Who was he? Would she ever see him again? Where would he be?

There was no way she could forget him. He was too deep inside her already. Even if she never saw him again she would remember him for the rest of her life. The idea that she'd never see him again felt desolately tragic. What she'd felt with him, could she ever feel anything like that with someone else? She seriously doubted it.

Sabra didn't have to argue with herself about what she was going to do. The arguments in her mind didn't make a dent. She would go out tonight and search for him. She had to. She was compelled beyond reason. The desires of the animal inside her took over with fierce primal instinct.

The entire day stretched out before her. The morning sunlight streamed through her window, bringing with it the acidic reality of what her day would consist of. Tucker and Gahu would be spreading the word around about their deal. She was bought and paid for with a ticking clock over her head. The Savage Solstice was her deadline to become the fighter she had to be, and to change her fate. She would never be content to stand quietly behind Gahu. She damn well wouldn't do it. Especially now. She thought of the black wolf again.

She closed her eyes. His gaze ate her up as he moved in. Heat rushed up her body, pulling chills behind it. Shivers and fever. She would find him again. He would drive her insane until she knew who he was. Once she knew, what would he do to her sanity then? She dozed into a mix of half-sleep, half self-constructed daydream.

She started guiltily as a knock sounded on her door. Reality sild down her throat with a bitter burn.

"Sabra! Get up and get dressed in your best dress," Tucker barked.

A few choice retorts ran through her mind. She *barely* kept them in.

"I can't," she said pathetically.

Tucker pounded on her door again. "Open this door right now!"

"Go away!" she moaned. "I'm sick. I'm not going anywhere. Go spread your happy news that you've roped Gahu into taking me off your hands by yourself."

"I don't believe you're sick."

"If I spew all over you will you be satisfied? Cause I'll be happy to oblige you."

"Damnit, Sabra! Why are you doing this? I know you're faking," he insisted.

"Maybe I am. Maybe I'm not. Either way, you don't want to take me along. Trust me."

"Why can't I count on you?" His voice went whiny.

"Oh, you can count on me. You can count on me to mess things up. It seems you think I always do. Just go away and leave me alone."

His exasperated sigh was so loud she heard it through the door. "Fine. But if I see you outside, looking well, you're in serious trouble."

"Noted. Now, go away."

She listened to him stalk away and slam the front door behind him. She thought about what he and Gahu would be saying about her. She imagined the hearty slaps on the back from the men and the hugs and congratulations from the women. Then she really did feel sick to her stomach.

She pushed her embarrassment down with anger and dropped to the floor, beginning her first set of push-ups, ignoring the pain of her broken rib. She'd burn off her emotions as she put her back into getting stronger. When she finished her workout, she didn't intend to stay in her room. Maybe she'd sneak off and run all the way to Paradigm. Asher's choice of training arena brought the shifters front and center in her mind. She wanted to learn what was happening to the shifters in the aftermath of Copernicus.

After she was sweaty and her muscles burned, she began thinking about what people would be saying about her. A familiar ache spread through her chest. Sophie. She missed her so much. She was so lonely without her. No one really knew her, now. Only Sophie had really known and understood the heart of her.

"I miss you, baby sister," she said aloud, quietly as if her sister could hear her. "You wouldn't believe what's happening to me. I'm going to be the pack leader. I swear I am. Tucker's got me locked up with some guy...and I met someone." Shivers ebbed and flowed on her skin as she thought about the black wolf again. "We ran together...something happened between us. It was elemental and...and hot. It's like there was light and flame all through me. I have no idea who he is, but what I felt with him was so *real*."

****

Shreve had watched Sabra use the whip as she fought with the older wolf in the ruins of the shifter colony. She looked like a vengeful goddess when she'd spun around and lashed out at that beam. He'd listened to their conversation. She was training for something. And there was a possibility she could die in the event. His stomach swooped as he witnessed her fighting ability. Her trainer didn't see her weaknesses the way he did, or if he did, he didn't say. Shreve could teach her better than that old man.

Stupid. He chided himself, instantly dismissing his idea. No, he couldn't train her. She'd never let him. But he didn't have to sit by and do nothing. He could help her.

He waited until the trainer put all the weapons back in their hiding place and left, before coming out. Just to be sure he wasn't caught off guard by anyone, he used his elf ability and became invisible before walking into the makeshift sparring ring.

He walked around it slowly, thinking. How could he make it a better training space for her? The charred earth under his feet drew his gaze and pulled his thoughts down like a magnet. Phantom screams of the shifters rose up from the ground and filled his ears. His stomach plunged, making him instantly and violently sick. He was a part of this crime. His hands hadn't lit the fires, or cut the flesh, but he'd delivered the order. He was the mouthpiece of evil.

Shreve found himself on his hands and knees. Guilt caressed from his head down to his feet with heavy hands. He tried to shake it off, but it clung to him and sank deep inside. He longed for forgiveness. The desire to run from this place filled him, but he knew better. There was nowhere he could go, nowhere to hide from the feeling inside.

Shreve felt the beating of his heart. Time thumping away. He would own his guilt. He wouldn't be a coward and waste the end of his life running from something he couldn't escape anyway. He took a deep breath and allowed himself to sink under the weight of self-hatred. He touched the ground and brought his dirt-covered finger to his tongue. He let the bitter granules rest in his mouth before swallowing. The dead were a part of him now.

"I won't ask for your forgiveness," he whispered. "I'm not worthy of asking. But I am sorry. No, *sorry* isn't adequate. I am broken with remorse. Everything I did...I had no right to do. And no matter the regret, I cannot reverse it...I can't take it back, even though I'd give anything."

He forced himself to his feet. There was nothing else for him to say to them. He couldn't do anything to help them. But he could help Sabra. He thought of his fleeting time left to live. *She's worth it. I'll give my time to her.*

He found the whip in its hiding place and pulled it out. He tucked the coiled leather under his arm and left the blighted place. He'd return it before she came back again. After he'd improved it.

CHAPTER FIVE

Tesla was down for her afternoon nap. Forest dug in the dirt around the plants under the open nursery window, enjoying the sunlight on her shoulders. The last few days had been a little easier. She didn't feel quite so ragged. Every time her mind began grinding on the wizard problem, her father being off-world, or her fear of Tesla's development, she would jerk herself up and put those worries in a cage. If catastrophe was looming, time was too short to waste it worrying on things she couldn't fix. She chased peace down until she caught it firmly with both hands. She had so many happy things in her life, she determined to focus on them, and let the rest fade to black.

She'd been so isolated the last few months. She had meetings scheduled tomorrow in her office. Syrus was taking the day off to let her go in to work. She missed her friends—Kindel, Ena, and Redge. She wanted to take Tesla with her and show her off, but she feared the baby would burn everyone with her hands. Forest didn't expect to be able to stay a full day in Fortress. She decided to begin to let a few people come to her home and meet with her there.

She desperately wanted some girl time with Netriet and Journey. She missed Shi like an aching hole in her chest, but Shi was silent now, not gone, but inaccessible.

Something's wrong.

Ice and steel went straight down her spine, and she held her breath, listening. There was no noise for a moment. Forest got to her feet and rushed into the house. Tesla screamed before she reached the nursery door. Forest flung the door open and ran headlong into an electrical storm. The force of the energy in the room threw her backward. Red sparks and lightning snapped and flashed over the crib, filling the air around Tesla.

Forest pushed at the energy holding her back, but it wouldn't let her through. *Syrus!* She yelled for him in her heart.

He was behind her in three seconds. "What's wro—" He didn't finish his question, as he could clearly see for himself.

Syrus put both of his hands straight out in front of him and pushed into the dancing and flashing light that now filled the whole space. Lightning from his hands broke through the storm. Forest followed on his heels, desperate to get to Tesla. Syrus swept the energy away from the crib like spider webs. He reached in and picked the baby up.

He turned to Forest, his face drained of color and his mouth open in shock.

She shook her head in denial. "No. How is this possible?!"

"I don't know."

Tesla held out her arms for her mother. But she wasn't the four-month-old baby Forest had put to sleep in her crib only an hour ago. Somehow, in the electrical storm she created, Tesla had aged, so she now resembled a two-year-old. The baby outfit she'd been wearing hung in torn ribbons on her body.

Forest took her daughter in her arms and tried her hardest not to cry, but she couldn't help it. She sat in the rocking chair, and Tesla, who couldn't even sit up by herself earlier, sat upright on her lap. She held her little hands clasped together in her lap and wrung them slowly, the red veins still brightly lit from her fingernails stretching halfway up her forearms. Her black hair hung in unruly curls to her shoulders. Her large, gray eyes, looked calmly at her stunned parents. She was even more beautiful than before.

"Sweetheart, can you understand me?" Syrus asked her.

She nodded easily.

"What happened to you? Do you know?"

Her eyes widened, and she looked down at her hands. Tesla looked into Forest's face, strain pulling in her neck and around her eyes. She touched her lips, tugging her bottom lip to the side. A strange, strangled gurgle came out of her mouth. She balled her hands into fists. She threw herself backward, another odd sound coming from her throat. Tears began running down her cheeks.

Late that night, Forest sat alone in the garden, her head resting on her knees. So many fears and what ifs were spiraling through her mind. She heard Syrus come up behind her, but she didn't look up. He tapped her shoulder with the bottom of a full wine glass.

She sighed and took the glass gratefully from his hand as he sat down next to her.

"She's playing in her room," he said. "I left the front door open so she can find us if she looks."

Forest glanced at the door standing wide open, the light spilling out along the ground. Her burning, bloodshot eyes began filling with tears again.

"In one moment, I was robbed of two years... This morning I had a baby. Now I have a toddler." She took a deep drink. "I'd bring Copernicus back to life, just so I could kill him again."

He rubbed her back. "I would too."

"Do you think she can travel through time?"

He frowned. "I don't know...I hope not. I'd say it's impossible, but that's wrong, just because I've never heard of anyone who could. I don't think that's what happened today."

She looked desperately into his eyes. "What do you think happened?"

"I honestly don't know. I just hope it doesn't happen again."

"She can't talk, Syrus."

"You don't know that. She can't, *yet*. Give her some time to learn." He kissed her temple. "Don't buy trouble, baby. We've got enough already."

"I'm sacred...and I'm so angry."

"Just don't let her see any of that," he said.

Forest nodded and downed the remainder of her wine, trying to find something positive to think on. A small smile curved the side of her mouth. "Can you believe how gorgeous she is?"

Syrus grimaced. "Yeah, I can believe it. She's almost as beautiful as you."

Forest snorted and stood, the wine going pleasantly to her head. "She's much more beautiful than me."

He scooped her up into his arms and kissed her. "Don't say things like that to me. I'm going to have nightmares as it is."

"We shouldn't be out here like this. I think one of us should be with her at all times, at least for now."

He took her hand, and they both went back into the house.

Tesla was still small enough to sleep in her crib. Forest couldn't leave her side for even a minute that night. She sat on the floor, leaning against the crib slats, her hand stretched through the bars, resting on Tesla's back. Occasionally, she dozed, lightly. But she was always aware of even the slightest change in the rhythm of her daughter's breathing.

Syrus came in and checked on them throughout the night. He offered to take her place, but she couldn't leave. She knew she wouldn't be able to rest at all. She'd be more worried in the other room. At least here, uncomfortable and worn out, she felt Tesla breathing. It brought comfort of the most basic, naked kind. Tesla was alive. At the moment, that was the only thing Forest knew for sure. But of course, that fact could change. She had never felt the fragility of life as she did now.

Forest's hand moved gently back and forth on Tesla's back, feeling the structure of her little body, skin, flesh, and bones. She gazed at her sleeping face. Her cheeks were flushed, and her dark hair tumbled across her forehead. She was like a piece of fine china. That was how Forest thought of her: tenuous.

****

Journey slowly approached the Heart. She stayed outside the circle of crystal trees, in case the flame turned temperamental again. Redge had insisted on coming with her. She consented on the condition that he keep a *really* good distance away.

She closed her eyes and took a deep breath, lifting her hands and opening herself up fully to the Heart. "I'm back," she whispered.

Excitement shot through her as the flames trembled and sparks snapped around the top.

"I'm sorry for being too forceful the last time. I meant no disrespect. I'm an outsider. It was not my intention to cross a forbidden boundary. Please forgive me."

The wind blew inside the circle, the leaves chiming a heartbreaking tune.

"I'm a healer. A heart-reader. Will you let me in? Will you let me try to heal your heartache?"

The wind stopped. The music of the leaves quieted.

Journey sat on the ground, placing her palms flat on the soil. She waited. For a moment nothing happened. White light surged out from the base of the flames, running along the ground on the roots in the dirt toward Journey. The light grabbed hold of her hands and wrapped around her fingers, pulling her down firmly to the ground.

She tried to not be afraid. *Tried*.

The Heart pushed inside her again, like it had the first time. Journey felt clogged with it. Her lungs, her veins, felt too full to function. She exhaled, forcing herself to relax and give it space to nudge its way through. *The Heart* was reading *her*, but it gave nothing of itself in return.

Alien, the Heart whispered in her mind. Its voice was a mixture, male and female, dulcet and guttural at the same time. Journey found the voice beautiful and ethereal. *You are not Regian. Beautiful Alien. I like your flavor. Your power is seductive. I want to answer its whispering lure.*

Slowly, like thick liquid, the Heart retracted. The power and light holding to her hands vanished.

She breathed deeply a few times, now that she could fully fill her lungs again.

"Thank you… Will you let me inside you, now?"

No…perhaps next time. If you come back, I will want to taste you again. The love in you is intoxicating. It distracts me.

"Distracts you from what?" Journey asked.

Them. The flames reached out and caressed the crystal tree that was cloudy. *They hurt me so.*

"Who are they?"

The flames sparked around the edges again.

They are the ones who poisoned me. Their love was the catalyst of so much death. The Heart gave a soul deep sigh. *I love them so much. And I hate them, also.*

"Will you tell me?"

Lay your head on the ground and close your eyes. I will show you.

Redge was pacing, a worried frown etched in his brow when Journey finally came back to him. Her eyes felt raw and scratchy from tears. She pulled tight against his chest.

"What is it?" he asked.

She just shook her head. "Take me home."

CHAPTER SIX

Shreve was getting familiar with the wilds near the Lair, close to the Wolf's Wood. Apart from where the shifter colony used to be, no one cleared the forests, or lived there. Not that he was complacent or thought that he was alone. There was a road, infrequently traveled, as far as he could tell. He found the deepest, wildest place he could, where a river flowed not far away, and claimed the space for himself. The most important thing about his location was it was near where Sabra had shifted into a wolf. If she came back, he wanted to know immediately. His plans to pose as a werewolf and join their community were all but forgotten.

He laid the whip out on the ground in a straight line and considered it. It was completely inadequate. Sure, he could improve it, but in his current location, only marginally. There were a number of places he could go to find what he needed, but that meant time if he didn't open a portal.

He coiled the whip back up, seriously considering just sending himself to Paradigm to buy what he needed. Perhaps the fear that using his abilities would wind down his fleeting time faster was nonsense.

The fear remained as he argued with himself. He couldn't help Sabra survive if he was reckless with his time. No, he wouldn't open a portal. He owed her. He wanted to pay his debt, despite the amount was more than anything he could ever do. He'd let her sister die. Nothing he did now could bring her back. Nothing could erase the pain of losing her sibling.

Shreve looked up. The boundary of the Wolf's Wood wasn't far away. He could find what he needed there, most likely.

Yet he feared going in there. He feared facing Shi. He'd never interacted with her. All he knew about her came from what Copernicus had told him. He thought of her as a mirror. She might show him the truth of himself. She would condemn him to himself.

It was cowardice, he acknowledged, adding that flaw to his mental list of things he was learning about himself. Shreve frowned, trying to think the way other people, *good* people, thought about themselves. When good people learned unsavory things about themselves, was that it? Did the flaw determine their life journey? He thought about Forest and the time he'd spent tailing her, watching her. What he remembered helped him through his thoughts.

It was *right* to fight against the bad things you found in yourself, and *wrong* to let them lead, or conquer you. He knew this must be extremely basic in the ways of morality, but he tried to not be ashamed of his beginner's grasp of right and wrong.

So how did he conquer his fear of going into the Wolf's Wood?

Shreve walked forward as he thought. His desire to help Sabra was stronger than his fear of facing Shi. He picked up his pace.

Shreve ducked under the low-hanging branches of the monumental trees that lined the perimeter of the Wood. The last time he'd been here, he was following Copernicus to kill Maxcarion, with a line of assassins on his heel. And that was exactly where he was headed now. To Maxcarion's magically hidden home.

He walked slowly, using his elf blood to go invisible, in case people lingered around. His stomach felt hard inside as he worried, waiting for Shi to appear, or to speak to him in his mind.

She didn't. He waited for it, continuing to move forward on the dirt path, covered in shadow sand.

Nothing. Not even the feeling of being watched. He felt totally alone in the Wood. He'd been prepared to face her, but now that it seemed he wasn't going to, he exhaled in relief. He kicked a small amount of sand into the air, but it didn't bother him in the slightest.

Now that his anxiety was gone, he focused on where he was going. It wasn't too hard to remember the way. He made a few small wrong turns, but he was going in the right direction. There was something Maxcarion had left behind, a faint hint of residual power lingered after his death. Shreve's wizard DNA felt it clearly, and the feeling guided him to the right place.

The illusion that hid the doorway was half broken. Part of the magic remained, so the entrance peeked through here and there, patchy like missing scales on a reptile. It was still hidden enough, that you might not see it, if you weren't looking.

The rock entrance itself was broken, but there was a door beyond that. He pushed it aside and walked into the dark space. It was a mess. Stuff was strewn about and shattered on the floor. His heart began racing with excitement as he realized just how much was left behind, in spite of the fact the place had obviously been looted.

On the far wall stood a shelf lined with bottles of various colored liquids. Most of the bottles were fully intact. He recognized the wizard language on the spines of some of the books. Trinkets and artifacts from the wizard's world, and many other worlds, lay about on the floor among broken glass.

His mind settled onto his task of the whip. He needed to clean up the space first. The remaining magic called to his wizard blood and made him feel stronger. He stretched out his hands and sent a small surge of his power into the mess. The floor cleared of debris, the broken glass went soft and collected back together in a lump before re-hardening.

Shreve's heart thumped painfully fast in a warning. He dropped his hands. He'd have to finish the job through actual labor. He didn't mind.

An hour later, the place was clean and halfway sorted. He piled the broken furniture just outside the door, intending to burn it at the onset of evening. He kept the mat that had been on the bed frame, and a chair had survived, suffering only a few tears in the upholstery. A shard of mirror the size of his palm caught his attention in the stuff on the floor. He picked it up. Copernicus looked back at him. He glared at his reflection before looking closer. He could make his face into anything he wanted. What he really wanted was for his face to just be, without effort or alteration. He set the mirror down. He'd keep it, for now.

He surveyed the room. All in all it was a comfortable space. A place to sleep, hidden from most of the world, and best of all, it was close enough to Sabra. Shreve frowned as he analyzed his thoughts. He wanted to help her survive. He owed her. That was all. He tried to shrug off the uncomfortable fluttering in his stomach as he thought about the moonlight on her long hair, falling over her bare skin. What was this feeling inside him? He found it troublesome. Almost pain, a longing, and a pressure that begged release, while his mind was caught on a loop of the details of her. Her lips, her hair, her skin, and the wonder of what it would be like to touch and taste her.

He tried again to shake the feeling. He laid the whip out on the floor and began working on it. With only a few adjustments, he would transform it from a tired and mostly useless weapon, into something formidable.

****

Sabra spent more time than she'd intended working out. By the time she felt she couldn't lift one more thing, hours had passed, and she was too late to slip away and make it to Paradigm and back before Tucker noticed. In the late afternoon, she watched and listened to her people from her window, as they moved about the square. Nothing official was happening, but people always came to the square to swap gossip or trade goods. She caught a conversation about her.

"I guess she won't be fighting after all."

"Not now. Gahu won't permit it... Plus, I heard he's going to fight."

"Wow! Can you imagine mates against each other like that? To the death. That would go down in our history."

"I don't know if that would be romantic or twisted and sick."

They laughed.

"I'm really disappointed," a girl said. "I thought she would be the one to change things for us. But even she's submitted to a man. I guess this just proves that none of us has a hope of free choice. We're property, and we'll continue to be bought and traded."

An older woman patted the girl on the shoulder. "There are still good things to be had in life."

The young woman's face flushed red. "My father told me my time is coming next spring. I'd rather die. I think about committing suicide every night."

Sabra looked closely at the girl, but she couldn't tell who she was from her vantage point. She turned away from the window and left her room, so she couldn't hear any more of what was said outside. They thought she had caved, given up at the snap of a man's fingers. She understood it looked that way. She thought about what this new public perception would mean. At first, she wanted to scream through her window and tell them all nothing would stop her from fighting. But now...

As the evening blossomed through the sky, Sabra did something she had never done. She willing made dinner for Tucker. So when he came home, the smells of his favorite food met him.

He smiled broadly when he smelled it, but then his face fell comically as he looked at her. "What's gotten into you?" he demanded. "I thought you were sick."

"I was. But I'm much better now. Is Gahu going to come by tonight? I made extra."

He narrowed his eyes in suspicion when she pulled his chair out for him. He sat down slowly, looking at his plate of food as though it might be poisoned. She held her laugh inside and sat down next to him. If she played stupid, he'd grow even more suspicious. He was a dumbass, but he wasn't that foolish.

"Look," she leveled with him. "I'm trying to say sorry for the trouble I've given you. You don't have to look at the food with fear in your eyes. See?"

She grabbed her fork and took a bite off of his plate, and then she took a drink of his wine.

"Okay," he said slowly. "I'm still confused. Who are you, and where is my sister?"

"I'm adjusting to the idea of mating with Gahu. He's a good guy. I like him. I appreciate you're not just handing me over to anyone. Really, I do." And she honestly did appreciate it. "Is he going to come by or not?"

"He said he was." Tucker took a bite and gave an approving noise in his throat. "This is good."

She waited quietly while he ate. When he began his second helping, Gahu knocked on the front door. Sabra got up and went to let him in. He held out a single pink flower to her and smiled.

"Thank you."

"Are you feeling better? You look all right...more than all right."

"Thank you," she said again. "I'm feeling much better. Please come in. I've made dinner, if you're hungry."

He came in and sat down at the table across from her. He exchanged meaningful looks with Tucker as she served him, clearly surprised and pleased by her actions. Her smile began to ache around the edges. Gahu gazed at her on and off while he ate, hungry heat in his eyes. She looked away from him, blushing demurely, causing him to smile broadly.

When the men were finished eating, she took their plates away and didn't return to the table. Instead, she seated herself on the couch and put her nose in a book. They spoke openly next to her as though she wasn't there, or couldn't comprehend what they talked about. She turned the pages in a timed manner, not reading at all.

Tucker didn't bother thanking her for dinner before excusing himself and going to his room. Gahu sat down on the couch next to her. He wrapped his arm around her shoulders and pressed his thigh against hers. She closed her eyes and took a very slow breath as he began running his fingers lightly on her forearm.

She closed her book and set it down. He took that as an invitation, leaning in and pressing his lips to her neck. She didn't move.

"Was dinner to your liking?" she asked flatly.

He pulled back looking at her closely. "Very much. It's a pleasure you know how to cook."

Oh, the things she wanted to say and didn't. Instead, she smiled thinly.

"So, you and Tucker told everyone about our impending mating?"

"Yes. I was sad you weren't by my side. Were you really sick? Or did you just not want to be there when the news broke?"

Sabra raised her eyebrows, and then nodded. Point to Gahu. "I was sick. But I think it might have been brought on by nerves... The thought of telling people, well, it makes me embarrassed. I know how men talk at such times."

He scowled. "Are you...innocent?"

She blushed brightly. "Of course I am! Why would you even question that? Did you believe differently?"

She stood, but he grabbed her hands and pulled her back down next to him. "I'm sorry. I don't know what I thought." He smiled and kissed her mouth. "It makes me so happy to know that I will be your first."

"And last," she added.

"Yes, that, too."

She looked away from him again. "Are you going to respect the ceremony date?"

He sighed and crossed his arms. "I certainly don't want to."

"If anyone found out, it would publicly disgrace me."

"No, it wouldn't. You're mine, now. Everyone knows. There would be no disgrace."

"You don't understand. *You* wouldn't be disgraced. The other women would be harsh to me. I wouldn't be able to live it down. They would be relentlessly cruel. The Savage Solstice is a ways off. If you got me pregnant, I could be showing at our ceremony." Her voice shook. "You wouldn't do that to me, would you?"

He pushed off the couch. "You're killing me. I wanted to have you tonight. I thought I would."

Her shoulders shook along with her voice. "You must do as you wish. I will accept it." She looked up at him with wide-eyed horror.

He looked affronted, and then his expression changed, and he laughed. "Oh, stop that! I'm not going to force you. I'm not sure what's gotten into you, or who you've been talking to, but the physical act is really nothing to get so worked up about. You just need to trust me to teach you."

"If it's not something to get worked up about, why can't we wait?"

"Hmm...touché. Fine. I'll wait. For a while. But I'm not going to promise to wait until the solstice."

She blew out a relieved sigh, stood, and wrapped her arms around his neck. "Thank you." She kissed him softly on the lips.

He looked down at her, his brown eyes going feral. "I better leave before I break my word, just as I've given it."

She let go, and he turned on his heel and left. She retreated to her room and leaned her back against the door, exhaling in relief. Her eyes finally enjoyed the roll she'd kept chained, and she made a mock gagging noise in her throat. *Idiots*. Both Tucker and Gahu. Oh well, so far so good.

Not everything she'd said had been a lie. She *was* a virgin, but she wasn't the blushing flower she'd acted. Wolf men were ignorant to their women. Yes, she was innocent, as she'd said, but she was also a she-wolf, not some cold, debutante vampire. An animal lived inside her that taught her plenty. And Gahu didn't put her system on edge. Not like the black wolf did.

Finally, finally it was full night. Sabra waited until she knew Tucker was asleep before slipping silently out into the dark again. Time for her to just be herself. She ran for the joy of running, her body buzzing with excited chills. Could she find the black wolf again? Would he be waiting? Would he show her who he was in man form? Not knowing his identity was driving her crazy, like an itch she couldn't reach.

****

Shreve finished with the whip and walked through the darkness, to the shifter colony to put it back where it had been. The remains of the colony looked eerie in the moonlight. The burnt skeletons of the homes reached up, in a twisted dance of stillness. His heart sank again as guilt resurfaced, just as heavy as before. He shoved the emotion back. All he was here for was to return the whip.

He laid the coiled leather back in its hiding place. He smiled to himself as he imagined how she would react when she saw what he'd done to it, when she held it and experienced the change. He slunk back through the forest, the smile still fixed on his lips, just as she was fixed in his mind.

He thought about how she'd looked in the moonlight, before she shifted. He imagined touching her bare back with his palms. A shiver rose on his skin. *Fool. As if that would ever happen.*

Shreve stopped short. Sabra was near, he could hear her heart as she ran. His gaze dragged deep through the shadows, searching. There. He went invisible when he spotted her. It wasn't like before. She wasn't running very fast. None of the agitation she'd had before emanated from her aura. Instead, she gave off an excited, hopeful energy.

She slowed to a walk, turning her head from side to side, searching. What was she looking for? Him? He didn't dare hope.

Her head whipped around to exactly where he stood, still and invisible, as though she could see him. She cocked her head to the side and frowned, taking a step toward him.

"Hello?" she whispered. "Are you there?"

He didn't answer. He didn't move. She shook her head and turned away. He followed. She ran her fingers through her hair and sighed, looking up at the moon.

"I'd hoped you be here..." Her voice was quiet. "I dreamed about you. I've never...never felt like that before. The way I did with you. It was like...like I've never been myself quite to that extent before. Just being next to you woke things inside me."

His pulse thumped loudly in his ears. He was sure his heart would burst. She paced back and forth, her head thrown back, eyes closed. He moved closer. Close enough to see the goosebumps on her skin. She sighed again, rubbing her hands on her forearms. Then her hands moved up to her neck, she touched her lips, and then raked her nails along her scalp, through her hair. It seemed like she was imagining something. His hands on her?

"I want to know who you are," she said. "I want..."

He held his breath, waiting for her to tell him what she wanted, dying to know what she wanted, but she didn't finish her sentence.

"I imagine what you look like as a man. I hope I meet you soon."

She opened her eyes and looked around again. He was almost close enough to reach out and touch her. She scrubbed her hands over her face and shook her head. She looked back toward the Lair and began walking toward it. Panic filled him. He couldn't let her leave like that. He shifted.

She walked swiftly, but he caught up in a second, nudging the back of her leg with his wolf snout. She jumped in alarm and yelped. As her eyes fell on him, she smiled. Her smile broke his heart in a thousand pieces.

"There you are. Won't you shift back? Show me who you are?"

He barked once, turned, and trotted off. He glanced back, waiting for her. She frowned at him.

"This or nothing?" she asked.

He barked again.

She stripped down, brazenly, facing him. This time it wasn't his heart, but his head that threatened to burst open. She was perfect, exquisite, and overwhelming. There was laughter in her eyes. She was taunting him on purpose with her flawless body and glowing skin. She trembled as the shift moved up and over her. She charged at him in her wolf form, pouncing him down with her front paws, biting him on the back of the neck before running flat out through the trees. He charged after her, intoxicated by the deep connection that pulled between them again, as it had the first time.

For Shreve, it was like the most beautiful dream he could have ever had. They raced again, running next to each other. Sometimes their sides touched. She delighted in his company. Feeling her value him made him surge with an emotion he didn't have a name for, because he'd never felt such a thing before. She became the center of gravity.

After only a short time, she began to tire. He slowed down, concerned. She stopped and looked him in the eyes. Depth and wonder beyond words flowed between them. Her very presence humbled him. Then the guilt rushed in again. He was the lowest blackguard. She was a luxury...a comfort...a heaven he had no right to even consider, let alone touch.

She wanted to know who he was. He could tell her. That would get rid of her faster than anything else. She shouldn't spend her time with him, or even think about him. He should release her and let the fantasy fade away. That would be the right thing to do.

She moved in and rubbed against him. Then she lay down on the ground and rested her head on her paws. He felt just how tired she really was. She was totally vulnerable next to him, and that fact pushed his emotions even deeper. Why did she trust him? Did she see or feel good things inside him with this odd, animal connection?

She sighed, her body relaxing against his. He sank down by her side. He knew the exact moment she fell asleep, because that was also the moment his heart ran away without looking back.

He watched over her, not that there was anyone or anything to guard against. He guarded her anyway. She slept just one hour. When she woke, her tiredness seemed even worse than before. He walked next to her, back to where she'd left her clothes.

She shifted back into a woman and dressed quickly, her back to him this time. She yawned as she faced him again.

"I'm sorry. I'm exhausted. I need to go home." She smiled saucily. "I don't suppose you'd care to shift into a man and come home with me?"

A low growl rumbled in his throat without his consent. She seemed to understand the nuance and threw her head back and laughed.

"There's no point in being cagy, not since we've run together. I've already felt it all. Everything you'd be inclined to hide from me." She leaned down, bracing her hands on her knees, and looking him in the eyes. She raised her eyebrows in question. "Not gonna do it, huh? Not gonna show me who you are?"

He'd never felt such strong temptation. He turned and ran from her into the shadows.

"Until tomorrow night then," she called after him.

He ran in wolf form all the way back to the Wolf's Wood. Once inside the protection of Maxcarion's home, he shifted back into a man. His back pressed against the wall for support, his head in his hands, his heart racing. What was happening to him? What was she doing?

It felt like he couldn't breathe, but when he clutched at his throat, found he was breathing easily.

"She's not for you," he said aloud to himself. "It's nothing. Chemistry. Unthinking, unreasoning, heartless chemistry. She's not for you. She hates you. She hates who you really are. What do you care anyway? Damnit! You're dying!"

He sat down on the chair, his head still in his hands. He couldn't see her again. It was *wrong*. Right and wrong assailed him. He tried to think about it logically. The chemistry wasn't one-sided. She felt it, too. *She* came out into the night looking for *him*. But she wouldn't have if she had any notion she was consorting with her enemy. Spending time with her was like lying, because if he continued, he'd have to continue hiding who he was.

Wrong. It was most definitely wrong. And if she began to really care about him, he'd hurt her. He'd already done that enough by not saving her sister. No. No more heartache would come to Sabra because of him. So that was that.

He lay down on the mat on the floor and closed his eyes. Nothing prevented him from dreaming about her, however. In his mind, she was right there with him.

She looked into him with the depth of her beautiful, purple eyes as he ran his finger over her bottom lip. He kissed her mouth until she was breathless, her eyelids half-closed.

"I love you," she whispered.

Shreve groaned. Pleasure and agony mixed together inside him. Maybe he shouldn't fantasize about her, after all. She was a fatal fever. He could close himself away from everything in this place and daydream about her until his heart expired. If he went down that road, he'd die before he could redeem himself.

CHAPTER SEVEN

Forest took Tesla outside to play in the garden in the warm morning sunlight. She toddled around for a few minutes. Forest sat down next to the flower bed and watched her. She hoped Rahaxeris would come back soon, so he could examine Tesla. Perhaps he would know what had happened when she aged two years in one day. Forest hoped he could do something to make sure that never happened again. Tesla came over and sat down next to her, so her little body was touching Forest's side. She stroked her hair and kissed the top of her daughter's head.

"Do you want to play in the dirt, sweetheart?"

She didn't seem too interested. Instead, she pointed to a white flower.

Forest picked it and handed it to her. "Pretty, isn't it?"

She took it in her red-lined hand and screamed. Her scream was filled with outrage, which she directed at her mother. Startled and taken aback, Forest tried to figure out what was wrong.

Red snaps shot into the flower from her hands, instantly turning the petals brown and withered. As she looked down at it, huge tears began to roll down her cheeks.

"Are you upset because I picked it?"

Tesla nodded, wails of heartbreak coming from her throat.

"Oh, honey. I'm sorry. It's okay. There's still more flowers growing. I promise I won't pick any more of them."

Tesla held the flower gently in both hands. Her power continued to shock and scorch the flower. Her cries were so grief-stricken, tears began forming in Forest's eyes as well. She stood and picked Tesla up, rocking her slowly back and forth, trying to soothe her.

She slumped against Forest and rested her head on her shoulder, but her body still trembled with tears.

"Here, sweetheart. Let Mommy have the flower. We can put it back in the dirt, and it can feed the other flowers. Okay?"

Tesla stopped crying and looked questioningly into Forest's eyes. Forest set her down on her feet.

"Look here, we'll dig a little around the base of these flowers and put this one under the dirt." Forest tried to coax her to help. "Can I have the flower?"

Tesla hesitated, and then held it out to her mother. Her hands shocked Forest as she took the withered flower. Tesla watched her lay it in the little hole and then cover it over.

"There. Now its life will give back to the others. Okay?"

Tesla looked at her like she'd just done something outrageous. She gave a little cry and moved forward, uncovered the flower and held it again. Forest watched, intrigued, as Tesla walked over to the fountain and laid the flower on the stones next to it. She put her cupped hand into the water and dripped it over the flower.

Forest's eyebrows shot up, impressed that she could know plants need water. How did she know that? Of course, putting water on a picked, electrically fried flower wouldn't do anything except make it soggy. But still...

Everything seemed to freeze around Forest in the next moment as she witnessed the impossible. Tesla extended her index finger, and a straight line of red energy pushed out, like a long, sharp fingernail and held still. The electricity didn't dance or snap, it looked like it solidified. With her *fingernail*, Tesla cut the stem open from the bloom down to the base. She leaned over it, squinting, her face two inches from touching it.

She touched the electric tip to the top of the water, bringing one drop away, clinging. She set the water drop on the open stem and shot a spark into it. The tiny drop spun into a sphere, red light illuminating the inside of it. She closed the stem back up, the electricity surging onto the seam, stitching it closed.

Tesla toddled back over to Forest, holding the flower out to her, a huge smile on her face. Winded, Forest took the flower. Tesla turned around and walked away, as something else caught her attention across the garden.

Forest looked down at the flower. It shivered, the brown turning back to white. The flower moved slowly but constantly, into full bloom, then the petals withered and fell off. The stem curled up in death, but then it stretched out again, budding, then blooming. Forest watched the flower die and be reborn three times in a row before her pulse slowed down slightly.

She glanced over at Tesla, now playing happily in the dirt, and then looked up into the sky. It would be a few hours till Syrus came home. Could she wait that long?

Forest continued to watch the flower throughout the day. It never stopped. By the evening, she could say it was the best day she'd had with Tesla since she'd been born, albeit shocking. When Syrus came home, she greeted him with a smile and huge kiss.

"You're much happier," he said, pleased. "How is she?"

"She's playing in her room. It's been *interesting* today."

"Oh?" He turned to go see Tesla, but Forest grabbed his arm.

"Wait. Just a second. I need to show you something."

Syrus examined the flower as it went through its lifecycle. Forest paced as he watched.

"Our daughter is Doctor Frankenstein."

Syrus frowned, concentrating. "Doctor who? Oh, right, I remember that silly movie you showed me."

"She brought the flower back to life!"

Syrus lifted a finger at her. "Hold up there. She didn't bring it back to life. She turned it into a...machine."

"What?!"

"Well, it's *sort of* alive, but it's an organic machine."

"Holy shit! Can *you* do that, you think?"

"Maybe. I've never thought to try such a thing. I don't know that I could." He looked closely at the flower again, his frown creasing deeper. "I wouldn't even know where to begin. And she just knew? Just like that? It was fast?"

"Yeah."

He handed the flower back to Forest.

"I'll look at it again later. Let's just try and forget about it for a few hours now and just be a family."

****

Asher arrived at the shifter colony two hours before dawn. Sabra should be there soon. He took the time alone to look around the space and think about how he could use what was left to create an obstacle course. He wanted to see how lithe and fast she could move.

The remains of the house he used to hide the weapons had a decent amount of stone blocks in its foundation. He could dismantle it and move them around. He walked over to it, but as he did, he noticed something that gave him pause. Footprints. He measured his own foot next to them. They weren't his prints. And they certainly weren't Sabra's. Had they been there before, and he just hadn't noticed?

He looked closer and followed the path the stranger had taken, right to his weapon hiding place. Asher did a quick inventory. None of the weapons were missing. He did a double take as his eyes passed over the whip.

"Good morning," Sabra called brightly as she came up behind him.

He turned and looked at her. "Someone's been here."

"Huh?"

"Look." He picked up the whip and handed it to her.

She gripped the handle and let the thong fall down loosely to the ground. The sunlight glinted off the sharp pieces of metal and glass now woven into the leather. A vicious metal burr clung to the very end of the whip. Spines jutted out in every direction from the burr like a sea urchin.

"Wow! This is awesome! Not just a weapon for show now, huh? Thank you. I'm a little nervous about practicing with it. I'm going to have to be more careful. Screw ups will cost me more now."

"Sabra, I didn't do this."

"You didn't?"

"No. Like I said, someone's been here."

She looked down at the whip, thinking. Then a smile pulled up one side of her mouth.

"This is a serious problem."

"Why is this a serious problem?"

"Because our spot has been discovered." He was agitated.

"Stop worrying. My enemies wouldn't come in here and make my weapons better, would they?"

"No, I guess not. But still, why would... Why are you smirking?"

"I know who did this."

"Who?"

She blushed through her smile. "My guardian wolf."

"Your what? Are you talking about Gahu?"

She laughed. "Gahu? No way!"

Asher shrugged. "Yeah. I guess he would just break all the weapons if he found this place... So, who are you talking about?"

She mulled over what she should tell him. Then a thought occurred to her that spurred her on. "I don't know his identity. Perhaps you know him. I've only seen him in wolf form. He has jet black fur with no markings and green eyes."

He rubbed the stubble on his chin. "No. I don't know anyone who's *all* black. My brother is almost all black. But he has a brown patch on his back, and his eyes are brown. I've never seen green eyes on a wolf."

She was disappointed he couldn't solve her mystery. "Oh well."

"You need to be careful," Asher admonished. "Certainly strange. An unknown wolf. Everyone I know, I've known my whole life."

She chewed the inside of her cheek. "I know. That's what I thought. I mean, we all live together."

"Well, there have been some who've gone off on their own in the past. Rogues are crazy, or they go crazy quickly once they leave the pack. We're not designed to live alone. We need each other. Sometimes, I wish that wasn't the truth, but it is... Are you sure he's actually a wolf? Could he be a shifter?"

"Hmm...maybe, but...no. I've run with him. We connected. A shifter can mimic but they can't communicate on that level. At least that's what I thought. Right?"

Asher shook his head. "No, that's right. They can't connect with us like that." He frowned at her then. "You've run with a stranger...that's really..."

"Slutty?" she offered defiantly. "I went running on my own. He crashed my private party."

His disapproving look vanished. "Oh. Sorry for implying."

"Don't worry about it. I'm ready to get going. How am I training today?"

"Did you work on your strength yesterday?"

"Yes, sir."

"Good. Keep that up. I can tell from the death grip you've got on that whip that you'd like to start with it. I'm going to back off. Let's see what you can do with the improvements your secret admirer made. Then, if you don't mutilate yourself, we should move on to the sword."

"Sounds good."

****

Shreve watched Sabra again with her trainer. The adjustments he'd made to the whip pleased her. He could see it in her body language and facial expressions as she wielded it around the space. She was a natural with the whip, impressively so. And she moved so beautifully with it, more of a dance than fighting. He couldn't take his eyes off her. He tried. Really tried.

He shouldn't be here. He'd determined to help her and nothing more. His intellect and desire went to war again. Helping was all he was doing. He was watching her fight to see where, exactly, her weaknesses were and to continue to think of ways to help her from afar. If nothing else, he was confirming the changes he made to the whip weren't too much for her to handle. Well, they weren't, so he should leave.

Not so fast. She would begin to practice with the sword next. He needed to witness her prowess there, or lack thereof.

As soon as she moved on to the sword, Shreve was glad he stayed. He couldn't help wincing. She had a long way to go before she would be effective against an enemy. Her trainer coached her on technique. Shreve didn't disagree with what the trainer said, but it seemed to have completely escaped his notice that she was using the wrong sword. She was too short for the broadsword she was trying to wield.

She was too elegant for the clunky blade. He thought of the next thing he would do to help her. But it would have to wait till they were long gone. *And*, he thought, not too late at night so he could avoid her if she came out to run with him again. If she caught him on his way, he knew, without a doubt, he didn't have the willpower to resist her. And he must.

When the morning lightened the sky, they packed it in, and she left. He watched her go, regretting his voyeuristic time was over for today. The trainer lingered. He moved slowly. Seemingly doing nothing at all for a while. He placed the weapons in a different house this time. Then he pulled a pipe from his pocket and banged it against his palm, resting his hip against the remains of the house's foundation.

Shreve didn't move. He watched the man closely. Something was off in his behavior. His body language clearly gave him away. He knew, or suspected he was being watched.

"I don't know your angle in this, stranger," he said in a low volume. "I'm guessing you're close enough to hear me. I appreciate you doing something to help Sabra gain an edge. She can use every advantage she can get. So, from what she's told me, I think I'm right in assuming you're trying to pursue her...I understand. I'm old, but I'm not dead. She's very desirable, not to mention unique. I'm trying to help her survive, and so are you, it seems. Why don't you introduce yourself?"

Surprised and moved by the invitation, and seeing no harm in it, Shreve pushed his elf blood back, dropping his invisibility. He did something he hadn't in years, and mixed two of his racial identities together. When he stepped out in the open, Asher confronted a part wolf, part shifter. Shreve created a new face for himself as a shifter, and the rest of him was werewolf. He didn't know what he looked like, but he didn't care, because he made sure he didn't look like Copernicus. He wondered why he hadn't thought of this before. He could pass as a Halfling, like Forest. And that would answer the question of why none of the wolves knew him. Because he'd never been to the Lair, having been raised by the shifters instead.

A pang hit him in the gut as he approached and thought of his cover story. *Lies.* What was this feeling? It was like the heavy guilt, only not quite so severe. Was it his conscience?

When the wolf spotted him, he straightened and gave Shreve a direct probing stare. He held his hand out in greeting.

"Asher," he said shortly.

Shreve shook his hand, trying to regurgitate a fake identity. It got lodged in his throat.

"What's your name?" Asher asked.

"I don't want to tell you." The truth came out.

"Why?"

"I'm a criminal."

Asher frowned, but he didn't recoil or lash out at him. Instead, he crossed his arms over his chest and continued to look directly at Shreve. "What was your crime?"

"You name it, and I've probably done it... But that was before. I'm not like that now. I want to be a good man. I'm trying."

"You changed Sabra's whip?" he demanded.

"Yes."

"Why? What's your interest in her?"

"I owe her a great debt. One I can never repay."

"Are you the one she's run with? The black wolf?"

"Yes. I have run with her."

"She doesn't know who you are, but you say you owe her a debt. Explain that to me."

Shreve swallowed hard. The truth was pushing to come out of him. But at what cost? There was something about this guy that made Shreve want to trust him. "If I tell you, will you promise not to tell her who I am, or that you've met me?"

"Give me a good reason to keep your confidence, and I will. I care about Sabra. I'll protect her. You, sir, are an oddity. Openly you tell me you're a criminal, one who's committed every sin, but that you've reformed... You're playing some kind of game with her, right? Trying to make her care about you?"

"I...I don't know what I'm doing exactly. I want to help her. To ease my conscience, I guess. Running with her wasn't anything I planned. It just sort of happened. Our paths crossed. I had no idea what that would be like... The connection. I never expected her to come back looking for me last night the way she did."

Asher held up his hand to stop Shreve. "Wait. You've run with her more than once?"

"Yes. As I said, the first time was just a happenstance. Then she came back out again, looking for me. I should have ignored her, I guess. But..."

Asher laughed. "But you just couldn't resist?"

"I couldn't. I don't want it to happen again... No, that's a lie. I want it more than anything. But I think it's wrong. I want to help her without interfering in her life any more. I watched you train her. She's got the wrong sword. The broadsword is too heavy. She needs a katana."

Asher raised his eyebrows and then nodded his head. "You're right. That would be much better for her. I don't have a katana though."

"I do."

"And you'd be willing to give it to her?"

"I'd give her anything."

Asher's gaze went even deeper. "You're all alone in the world, aren't you?"

"Yes. I suppose I am. It's better than the way it used to be for me...I'm not a threat to Sabra, or anyone else."

"I know that."

"How do you know?"

"Because you've run with her, *twice*. If there was any malice inside you, she would have been able to detect it easily. She wouldn't have sought you out a second time. That shows an inherent trust. So, I will go off that."

"How do you know I didn't fool her? I'm not just a wolf. Why haven't you asked me about what I am?"

"It's not *what* you are, but *who* you are, that I care about. And I've taken your measure myself. I'm old. The longer you live, the easier it is to spot assholes."

Shreve smiled. "And what of my past?"

"Well, I'm terribly interested, not gonna lie. But that's your business to share or not. I will press you for one thing, though."

"What's that?"

Asher smiled. "Your name."

His pulse hammered in his ears. He should never speak his name. But he'd confessed so much already. What did it matter? His heartbeat reminded him succinctly that he was dying.

"Shreve." He winced as he said it.

"I don't recognize your name, friend. Your reputation hasn't preceded you, at least not to me."

He exhaled, his pulse easing off its gallop.

"I was thinking about making this place more of an obstacle course for Sabra to train on," Asher said. "Would you lend me a hand?"

Shreve smiled again. "Sure."

****

Sabra was jazzed. Her muscles hummed with the excursion of training. She managed to sneak into her room and shut the door a second before Tucker got up. She was cutting it close, too close today. She needed to get up earlier tomorrow. Too much was riding on this. Just because her dreams were crazy hot, confusing, and prevented her from getting the rest she needed, she had to push through and get up.

She smiled to herself as she thought of how awesome her whip was now. Her wolf had given her a gift. It had to be him. When she went out to run with him tonight, she planned to force him to show her who he was.

Tucker banged on her door. "Sabra! Get up!"

"Okay," she grumbled, trying to sound like she was still half asleep.

The day was going to stink. Big time. She wasn't going to get out of seeing Gahu, or having him parade her around. She would have to smile and act happy at having been conquered. She mentally held on to the feel of her whip, like a safety blanket. When the day became overwhelming and vomiticious, she'd think about her whip and her mystery wolf. Her real life was not in the here and now of the Lair. It lay in the freedom of her own power and running in the wilds at night.

Her morning excursions clung to her in a funky layer. She bathed and got dressed. She surveyed her appearance in the mirror as she put the wooden cuff around her wrist. It was like a stranger looking back at her. This was Gahu's woman.

Tucker was already gone by the time she came out of her room, dressed and ready for the day. Her cheeks flushed and burned with humiliation as she thought again about what she was about to go through, once she stepped out into the open. Every bad word she knew ran laps in her head.

The morning sunlight was cool and bright. She meandered around the edges of the public square. Only a few people were there. They looked at her and then began whispering. She acted as though she hadn't noticed and looked down at her feet. That was a mistake. She didn't notice who was approaching until it was too late.

"Sabra."

She'd expected Gahu. Instead, she looked up into the satisfied face of Silhon.

He grabbed her wrist and held it up. "Look at this!" he exclaimed to his friends behind him. "She's been cuffed. Our would-be leader."

She pulled her wrist from his grasp. He stepped into her space, lowering his voice to a whisper. "I'm disappointed. I can't tell you how much I longed to kill you in the tournament." She felt him shiver. "The thought really turns me on. You better keep close to Gahu. I'm not happy about being cheated out of my desires. I'm not letting go of the idea, just because you've proven to be nothing but a woman wanting to hide behind a man. I still want your blood all over me."

She sneered. "Of course you do. I know why you hate me so much. I know you wanted me for yourself, tried to convince Tucker to hand me over to you."

His cheeks reddened. "Like I said. You'd better stay close to Gahu. If I find you alone..." He shivered again. "Oh, how I'm going to make you scream."

He reached around her and grabbed her ass. Her elbow connected with his mouth, and his head snapped backward. He roared, and his gang pressed in around her, caging her with their bodies.

"Back off!" Gahu yelled, striding toward them.

They parted and shoved her away. He stood protectively in front of her. Silhon wiped the blood from his lip and sneered at him.

"Keep a leash on your bitch, Gahu. Anyone might think she's too wild for you. If you don't break her soon, just think of the talk. No one will consider you a real man."

"I don't care what she did. She's mine. All of you, keep your hands off her. Or the tournament just might have to come a little earlier than planned."

Silhon laughed and pushed by them, his gang following in his wake.

She looked up into Gahu's angry face. "I didn't do anything. I swear. He came up to me and threatened me. He put his hands on me. Surely it's okay for me to defend myself."

"Of course it is," he said tersely. "Just stay away from Silhon, please."

"I'm trying to, he sought me out. Trust me, I want none of his society."

The anger eased off his face. He put his finger under her chin and tipped her head up, pressing a warm kiss on her lips. He took her hand and towed her along, ready, it seemed, to show her off as his property.

People gathered around them. It was just how she'd imagined, unfortunately. He was congratulated, and she was hugged by the older women, admonishing her to be submissive and to think about her future role as a mother. Their faces all blurred as her anger began poking sharply under her cool exterior. She took a deep breath, smiled, and thought about her whip.

One face came into focus through the crowd. A young woman was looking at Sabra as though she had just stabbed her in the back. She recognized her and realized she was the one who had been talking under her window yesterday, saying she'd rather die than be handed over to a man.

Sabra pulled closer to Gahu. "I'll be right back. There's someone I need to talk to."

"All right." He smiled jovially, clearly enjoying all the attention, and released her hand.

She moved through the crowd, locking eyes on the young woman. "Lynne, can I speak to you in private?"

Her eyes widened, but she nodded. Sabra threaded her arm through Lynne's and directed her away from the main crowd. She turned and looked severely into the girl's eyes.

She kept her voice low. "I just want you to know, no matter how this looks, I did not betray you or the rest of our women. I can say no more. Just know that things are not how they seem. Changing things is still what I am working for."

Lynne threw her arms tightly around Sabra's neck, surprising her. "Thank you!" she whispered in her ear. "Thank you so much!"

Lynne released her and walked away. The weight of the moment fell hard into Sabra's stomach. Everything she was fighting for was so much bigger than her. It wasn't just her fate and her future happiness that was on the line. She couldn't flinch away from the gauntlet before her. No matter what, she had to run through it. She looked back at Gahu. *No matter what.*

CHAPTER EIGHT

Merhl crumpled up the large sheet of paper he'd been writing on and threw it angrily to the floor. He rubbed his aching hands together and tried to focus, but he felt he might burst into frustrated tears. He was in the room Zeren had given him to use as an office inside the Onyx castle. The space was large with an ogre-sized desk on one side. He kept the rest of the room bare and used its dead space to experiment. He'd created lots of new things in the last few months. Many possible concepts to hold back the Wizards from entering Regia. But so far, he'd yet to hit on an idea that he felt confident would actually work.

He could create walls and portals that no Regian, not even Rahaxeris, could get through. But wizards...Zeren kept admonishing him not to lose hope, that *he* was Regia's best chance at survival. Maybe he was the most powerful Ogre, but he didn't have what it took to stop one wizard, let alone an army.

Merhl felt Regia's best hope was in Rahaxeris, that somehow he could solve the problem. They'd had many long discussions on the matter. He hoped Rahaxeris would come back soon with good news.

He pulled out a new piece of paper and took up his writing stylus again. The blank page was like a barren desert of death. His mind was as blank as the paper.

Someone knocked softly on the door.

"Yes," he said loudly.

The door creaked open, and Journey peeked around it. "Are you in the middle of something?"

He couldn't help but smile at her. "I wish. Come in."

She closed the door behind her and came toward him. "I have an idea."

He set his stylus down and gave her his full attention. "Good. Cause I've got nothing."

"I've been talking to the Heart."

His eyebrows shot up. "Really?"

"Yes. It spoke to me. I think it will again. It asked me to come back. I'm going tonight. I think...I hope..." She paused, fighting to get her thoughts to come out. "There is more power in the Heart than I could have ever imagined. I feel certain it is the reason the wizards desire to conquer Regia at all. They want the Heart...We have to figure out a way to use the Heart to protect us."

Merhl's mind began spinning on the possibility. "Of course! Brilliant!"

"I need some more time. The Heart is shy and fractured. If I can heal it. I think it will consent to whatever we need. The Heart *is* Regia, after all. There's a consciousness there I don't believe anyone else has been able to connect with the way I have. Not even the Dryads."

"So what do we do?"

"I'll tell you what I learn from our next conversation. I think you should think about the stuff you already know how to make, but with unlimited power behind it."

Merhl smiled. "You convince the Heart to play along, and I'll find a way to build the wall."

She touched his forearm, a frown creasing her lovely face. "You're worn down. I'm sorry I didn't notice until now."

"Did you just read me?"

"Yes. I could give you a story. It will rebuild your stamina and your hope."

"I'll take you up on that offer, Storyteller. But not right now. You've given me all the inspiration I need to keep me going the rest of the day. I already have a ton of new ideas."

"Excellent. Then I'll leave you to it."

****

Redge leaned against the wall, watching Journey get ready to go to see the Heart again. He was determined to go with her and wouldn't hear anything otherwise. She fastened her cloak under her chin and took a deep breath, looking at him. He gave her a small smile.

"Are you sure you really want to try this again?" he asked for the tenth time.

"Yes. I know how I'm going to approach it tonight. The history of Shi and Leramiun's tragic love is more than enough to begin with."

"You're honestly not putting yourself in any danger doing this?"

"Well, I can't say I'm one hundred percent sure. But I'm very confident nothing ill will befall me. I promise you. And you'll be close by, if I need you."

One of the castle's ogres opened a portal to the Wolf's Wood for them. They walked silently, hand in hand, till the manifestation was visible. Redge turned Journey to face him. He didn't say anything. He cupped her cheek and kissed her deeply before turning and walking off.

She approached the Heart slowly. The music chiming through the leaves of the crystal trees was a slow sleepy tune. Like a lullaby of the brokenhearted. As she came near, the charcoal flames sparked at the top, and the song ceased.

Journey sat cross-legged on the ground and placed her palms flat on the dirt as she had before. She didn't have to wait or coax this time. Light spread out from the base of the flames, running on the ground toward her. It grabbed onto her hands and held fast.

Beautiful Alien. You have returned.

"Are you ready to let me in?"

It hesitated. *If I let you in, will that be the end of our time together?*

"Not unless you desire it to be the end," Journey said.

I desire more time with you. I am intrigued by what might ensue with letting you use your power on me. I love your flavor, but I will refrain from absorbing you.

A small pang of fear shot into Journey's belly, but she pushed ahead. She'd been considering how she would go about this since the last time. It was uncharted territory. She closed her eyes, trying to push back on the light that held her. Not to free herself from its hold, but to reverse the flow back on the Heart. Gold light moved from Journey's hands and veined down through the white light holding her. The gold slithered toward the flames as Journey began to hum.

Her voice slithered along with the gold light, pressing closer. Journey felt like the ground vanished out from under her as the Heart pulled her inside it like an undercurrent. She was inside a metaphysical womb. Her spirit was engulfed from all sides, and she felt everything. Everything there was in existence to feel. All emotion, light and dark, holy and evil, and everything in between was there. Softness beyond anything she'd ever felt touched her, followed by murderous edges of rage. Ultimate passion and ultimate peace.

Momentarily winded, Journey fought to fill her lungs and tell the Heart a story. She sang of Shi and Ler, and the Dryads. The Heart eased around her, giving her its full attention.

She opened her eyes, but she couldn't see the wood anymore. Only colors and light. Journey looked all around as she sang. It was like being trapped in a dome of deadly textures. The space around her morphed back and forth. The brokenness, the poisoned places, were like gaping torn flesh, putrid disease visible under the surface.

Her voice reached out to everything in front of her, good and bad, and pulled it into her song. The Heart trembled in response to the story. The notes fell on the gashes like golden raindrops, absorbing into the wounds, pulling at the openness. The light attempted to bind the tear together like a stich. The womb around her convulsed once, and then gave a shallow sigh.

You have an amazing gift, Alien. You taste so good.

The walls around her turned to liquid, rushing on her, holding her.

Journey panicked.

"No! Please don't!" she begged. "Let me go! Please!"

The rushing stopped and retracted. *Don't fear, Alien. I won't end your life. The love you have for Redge needs to be. I won't separate you... Thank you for the medicine. I feel better. Will you come back to me and sing again?*

"Yes. I will come back."

The Heart pushed her out like a feather in a gust of wind. Journey felt the ground beneath her again. She opened her eyes. The wood jittered and blurred in her vision. The light on the ground moved away and back to the flames. For a few minutes, she just sat there, feeling her lungs fill and empty. Her vision cleared. The flames were different already. The charcoal color was swirled with a light purple.

Journey smiled and got carefully to her feet. She turned from the Heart and walked away, anxious to find Redge and tell him about her success. She found him in a few minutes. He was squatted down, looking intently at the ground.

"What is it?" she asked.

"Footprints."

"So? People come through here."

"Yes. I'm just looking. This area here." He pointed. "The dryad graveyard...the wizard used to live close by. He's dead now, but someone has been here recently. See?"

She looked. She didn't see much, not perceiving physical evidence the way he did, and impatient to tell him about her experience, she reached out and took his hand. "Do you see anything dangerous?"

He looked at her. "Not necessarily."

"Let's go home. You won't believe what just happened to me."

She pulled him away. He glanced back, instinct telling him to pay attention to his gut. There was someone of interest in the Wood. An enemy perhaps.

****

Rahaxeris sat in the blank grey queue, waiting his turn alongside a row of androids. He felt the pressure of days going by, but in this waiting place, time was deactivated. It had been many years since he'd been to Polyhedron. It was a world of living machines. Devoid of emotion, it ran on balance, logic, and numbers. He had no doubt the leader, Nero, would remember him. He also had no doubt that Nero knew everything about the wizard's plan and motives. He wasn't quite as confident that Nero would tell him what he needed to know.

One more android stood and left the queue. It would be his turn next, and he would have to plead his case concisely. It wasn't like him to be as emotionally distraught as he was. It was hard to focus on the logical arguments he might need to present to Nero, when he couldn't stop thinking about his daughter and granddaughter. He reminded himself that their lives rested on his ability. Just like a combination lock on a safe, he felt his cold nature click firmly into place.

The android who'd gone ahead of him came back through the door. Rahaxeris stood. It was his turn.

He walked steadily into Nero's seamless grey chamber. Nothing had changed since the last time he'd stood here. Not that he'd expected it to change. Nero sat in front of him, a beautiful shiny white android with large, liquid, black eyes. Blue lights and gears illuminated his chest and hands. The shape of his head stretched up and out, twisted around like the branches of a tree. Each white spire on his head also had a tiny blue light at the very top.

For lack of a better term, Nero was a king. But since he had no emotion and thus no ego, it wasn't necessary for Rahaxeris to bow, or make any show of groveling.

He simply inclined his head. "Nero."

"Rahaxeris of Regia. I knew you would come back sooner or later. What can I do for you?"

"The wizards..."

"Ah, yes. I know of that, and under no uncertain terms, condemn it."

Rahaxeris felt a spark of hope in his chest. "Then will you help us protect ourselves?"

"Of course. Take that," Nero said, pointing at nothing at all.

Before Rahaxeris could question, a white cube the size of a fist appeared and hung in midair in front of him. He reached out and took it. The material it was made of was unknown to him. It was solid and fluid at once. Deceptively heavy for its size.

"What is it?"

"A power harness tesseract. Don't get too excited. It's not total salvation."

"Is it a gift?" Rahaxeris asked.

"It is. I ask nothing in return."

"Thank you."

"Is there anything else?" Nero asked.

"Why are the wizards doing this?"

"Their entire plan, misguided as it is, is about survival, and an old feud among themselves. To put a finer point to it, it is about sex. The wizards are lifeforms with assigned genders and rely on their females for survival. They are not so different from any other male- and female-based people. The males are hard, and brutal. Their culture took a turn long ago that displeased their women to such an extent that they declared war. In their folly, the wizards almost annihilated all the witches. Those that survived took their daughters and left their homeland.

"Since there was no more procreation, the wizards set out to become immortal. They drained their world's natural power resources in their pursuit. In need of new power sources, they ventured out from their world, searching. This endeavor to conquer many worlds is based on the power sources they discovered.

"In comparison, all Regian races are feeble. It is the Heart of your world they desire to possess and consume."

Rahaxeris looked down at the cube in his hand. "I'm very grateful to you, Nero, for sharing this information with me, and for the tesseract."

"Use the tesseract in harmony with the Heart of Regia, or this hope I have given you will only add to your doom."

He gave Nero a little bow. "Thank you."

Nero nodded and flicked one of his shiny fingers toward the door, indicating his audience was over. Rahaxeris left the room and walked back through the waiting area, anxious to get home.

CHAPTER NINE

Shreve discovered another flaw in his character. When it came to Sabra, at least, he had absolutely no self-control. She'd said she was coming back the night before. He'd decided to not see her again, because it would be better for her. But it was easier to feel conviction in his decision in the morning when the night was still so far off. As the afternoon wore thin, his resolve was pushed to the back of his mind, and fantasies kindled and began to burn. Then, as it became evening, determination crumbled to dust, replaced by a fluttering excitement.

You can't do this, his guilty conscious insisted.

The desire was stronger than the guilt. He only wished he hadn't told Asher that he'd decided to not see her again. It felt terrible to go against his word. He hated lies.

He looked at Forest's sword clasped in his hand. Was it wrong to give it to Sabra? He sat down and sighed. Why was he so torn about everything? He'd meant to put the sword with the whip earlier in the day. He surely hadn't intended to introduce himself to Asher. But he was so glad that he had. The old wolf had integrity, and Shreve longed to call him a friend. He seemed willing to give Shreve a chance and not condemn or shun him for his past.

He rested his head back on the chair and closed his eyes. He should just stay here in Maxcarion's old home and not go out tonight.

But she was expecting him. He stood and strode out into the darkness, sword in hand.

He walked swiftly through the forest to where she'd been last night. The night was quiet. The only sound was the moving of the river in the distance. Perhaps it was too early for her to be out. He'd wait. What was he planning? Should he shift into wolf form now? He picked up his pace, walking toward the shifter colony. If he saw her tonight or not, he could leave the sword for her, so she'd have it in the morning.

He approached the house that served as her weapon's hiding place and heard her, only a second before she stepped out from behind the ruined house. She was in silhouette, but there was no mistaking those curves, it was her. His heart rose up to his throat and choked him. She held the whip, moving her wrist lazily back and forth so the end slithered rhythmically like a snake on the ground.

"Hello," she said quietly. "It's you, isn't it? My mystery wolf."

He couldn't move. This was the worst thing that could have happened. Now he'd have to speak to her. The only comfort he had was knowing she couldn't see him clearly in the dark. He shifted his face just in case her eyes were keener than he thought.

"I hoped to surprise you, so I could catch you in man form. Guess I have." He could hear the smile in her words. "It's odd, don't you think? I know you so well on one level, but I don't know your name, or anything at all about you."

"Yes," he managed, no louder than a whisper. "Sabra."

"How do you know my name? I didn't tell it to you, did I?"

He didn't answer. "I've brought you something. A sword better suited to your size than the one you used earlier today."

"You've been watching me more than I realized. I knew you had, obviously, by the fact that you messed with my whip. You did, right? It was you who changed it?"

"Yes."

She took a step toward him. He could see more of her features. Her gaze held fast to his. He had no idea what he looked like. Under her scrutiny, he felt a shiver move over his face, as if it shifted without his consent.

A small gasp escaped her lips. "How can it be? I must be dreaming."

"Why do you say that?"

94

"You look almost the same as you did in my dreams." She dropped the whip and reached for him.

"Stop!" His voice was rough.

Her arms fell to her sides, and she looked at him, confusedly. "There's something about you... something familiar, as if I've met you before... It's your voice... Who are you?"

"I can't tell you. I don't really know who I am."

"What's your name?"

He didn't answer her question. "I'm just trying to help you survive. Here."

He reached out with his left hand, grasping her arm gently above the elbow. His hand slid slowly down to her forearm and then her wrist. His thumb pressed into her palm, opening her hand. His right hand brought the hilt of Forest's sword to her palm. She wrapped her fingers around it as he let go and stepped back.

His hand curled into a fist, as if he could hold the sensation of touching her skin right there, imprinted forever. Now he knew what it felt like to touch her, but the knowledge was damning. It didn't satisfy; it made the longing worse. He wanted to touch all of her. He turned and walked away, while he still could.

"Please," she pleaded.

His heart tore and groaned in response to her voice.

"Please, tell me your name?"

He hung his head. She would have nothing but hatred for him when she wised up. Even still, he wouldn't lie. "Shreve," he managed quietly, letting go of the dream of her as he said it. He couldn't look back. He heard her step toward him, and he quickly walked away. "Goodnight, Sabra."

"When will I see you again?"

"You won't."

"It's not going to be that easy, Shreve," she called.

That stopped him. "What isn't?"

"Shaking me off... What are you running from?"

"The more time we spend together, it's just going to make it hurt that much more later."

"You're hurting already."

He turned around. "How would you know?"

"Tell me I'm wrong," she challenged.

He frowned and shook his head. "I can't. It would be a lie."

She took a step forward. "Look at me."

He did. After a second, he shook his head and backed away from her. "See? I feel like I'm drowning when I look at you, and all I want is to swim down. But you're not for me. Only pain comes with getting close to me. I don't want to hurt you."

Her smile flashed cruelly in the darkness. "You're right, I'm not *for* you. I belong to myself. And you, like all the others, think you could hurt me so easily. You've got it backward. The pain comes from me. I bring it. I make it. So if you're going to run, run because you're afraid of how *I* will hurt *you*. Not the other way around. And if you do run, don't ever come near me again. Just because I'm strong doesn't mean I want a man who's weak."

He listened to every word carefully. "I could never be what you need." He gave her a little bow. "Goodbye, Sabra."

He turned and walked away from her. This time, she didn't follow.

****

She watched the shadows swallow him up. This was all wrong. How could that have gone so badly? Her pulse boomed in her ears, and her lungs hurt as she breathed. She took the sword he gave her back to the weapon stash and laid it carefully with her whip. Her mind was momentarily numb.

For a few moments, longer than she thought, she just stood there in the moonlight, touching her arm, tracing where he'd touched her. Her skin still held the warmth. Shivers uncoiled through her. Despite what she'd said, he didn't strike her as weak. Not at all. He was *more*, more than she'd imagined, more attractive than any other man she'd ever met. She had been certain that she would be disappointed when she finally saw his face, after her dream version of him. Her fantasy had been close but, to her amazement, had come up inadequate to reality. He was like his wolf form. His eyes were a deep green and his hair was blacker than midnight. His features were strikingly wolfish, and his mouth... Mercy, she wanted to see him smile.

Heat akin to a fever rushed in her. She touched her eyes. They were dry, but for the first time since Sophie had died, she felt the sensation that she might cry. The pressure in her temples both confused and angered her.

"Yeah, we'll see," she said quietly, thinking he couldn't hear her. "I know how much you want me. I've felt it. We'll see how long it takes before you come back for me."

"Careful, Sabra." His voice came through the shadows. "The beast that lives in me is different than the one inside you. Don't tempt me so brazenly."

She held still, waiting to see if he would come back. He didn't. She turned and headed home, his words of warning on constant replay in her head. She grinned all the way home, the feverish sensation under her skin growing hotter. She'd seen his face. She knew his name. And she tempted him.

****

When Asher came to the shifter colony the next morning hours before dawn, Shreve was there, waiting for him.

"Hello," Asher said easily. "What are you doing here?"

"I have to confess something."

"Oh?"

"I broke my word. Yesterday, I told you I wouldn't see Sabra again."

Asher snorted and smirked. "Ah. And you did. Let me guess, you couldn't help yourself?"

Shreve's eyes lit up. "How did you know?"

"I was a young man once, too. Trust me, I understand."

"I talked to her." Shreve began to pace. "It was like…" He scrubbed his hands over his face. "I'm losing my mind, and I'm diseased, or something. It's like the most terrible torture, and I love it."

Asher laughed. "Like I said. I understand."

Shreve looked at him and sighed helplessly. "I gave her the sword last night."

Asher walked over to the stash of weapons and came back out with Forest's sword. He frowned as he looked at it closely, pulling it from its scabbard. He flicked his finger on the edge of the katana, making the silver ring. His gaze shot deep into Shreve.

"A product of your criminal days?" he demanded.

"Sort of."

Asher's expression grew hard. "Sabra will be here any moment. When she's done with her training this morning, I want to talk to you about this sword."

"You know it?"

"Yes. I do. I know who it belongs to."

"I'll tell you about how it came to be in my possession later, but so I can set your mind at ease and tell you now, Forest is my sister."

Asher's eyebrows shot up for a moment, then they came down in a scowl as he narrowed his eyes at him. "Hmm…" After a second, his expression smoothed. "I'm reminding myself of your openness thus far, and your affinity to confess things. *And* that I decided yesterday to trust you because my instinct told me to."

"Thank you."

"We'll talk later. Now get gone. I don't want you distracting my student."

Shreve smiled. "Are you sure distraction isn't what she needs to learn to fight through?"

He rubbed the stubble on his chin thoughtfully. "Maybe."

The sound of her approaching footfalls caught their attention.

"You think about it," Shreve said, turning and walking away.

He went to what was becoming his usual spot to watch her morning training and used his elf blood to turn invisible. She walked into the space, yawning. It was damn adorable. She muttered greetings to Asher as she bound her golden brown hair back.

Aching spread through his chest. It was getting worse. This feeling inside him, every time he looked at her. Every time he thought about her. Asher said he understood. How could he? What did that mean? He watched her as she began sparring with Asher.

Asher made her abandon the whip that morning and focus on the sword. She did better with the katana than the broadsword, as he knew she would. Asher sounded stern, and Sabra sounded arrogant. Their voices bounced in his ears, but he wasn't really listening to the words, until he heard his name.

His attention snapped up. Asher was facing his way.

"Shreve? Would you care to join us?"

****

Sabra froze. *Oh, shit! He's not serious, is he?*

Her heart stopped as Shreve stepped out from the thick of trees and into her sparring arena. In the predawn light, she could see him more clearly than she had last night. Heat rushed to her cheeks as he locked his eyes on hers. Never, *never* had she seen anything like him. Her whole body lit up and filled the air around her with a gravitational pull that reached out like a net trying to catch him. *Come to me. Touch me. You're mine.*

He moved toward her, obeying her silent summons. Asher seemed to disappear entirely.

"Hello, Sabra." His voice hit her sideways. She knew his voice. But from where?

He smiled down at her. She'd wanted to see him smile, but she hadn't really been prepared. Her racing, fevered brain crashed and held up a white flag. *I give up. He wins. I can't stand up against attraction of this magnitude. It's hopeless.*

Asher broke into her peripheral vision. He looked at her, and then at Shreve, and back at her again, a smug smile on his lips. "That took you down a notch, missy. If you're not going to listen to me, perhaps you'll listen to him."

Shreve and Sabra looked at him. "What?" they said simultaneously.

"Shreve is going to help train you. Isn't that right?" Asher looked pointedly at him.

"Oh... Yes. I'm going to help."

Sabra fought to pull herself together. "Really? What qualifies you?" she challenged.

He smiled again. She groaned internally. So not fair. How could anyone be so gorgeous? It should be illegal.

Shreve took a few steps back from her. "I guess there's only one way to prove it to you. Attack me."

"Oh, I'll *attack* you," she said, only her voice laced the words with innuendo and not the bravado she intended.

He raised one eyebrow, a small amount of surprise in his emerald eyes at the inflection in her words. She tried to school her brain. This was impossible. She couldn't fight him, she realized. Her mind raced along the reality if she charged at him. They would touch. His touch would scatter her focus, and he'd beat her easily, even if he wasn't a great fighter. It wouldn't work. The whole thing would just turn into foreplay.

She took a deep breath, stepped back, and looked at Asher. "I don't think this is a good idea. I'm sorry for being insolent to you. That was wrong of me. You've put me in my place. But he can't train me. It would be counterproductive."

"Oh?" Asher asked.

She scowled at him. These were the moments it sucked being a wolf. The animal side of them gave so much away. "I can't focus, Asher! There's too many damn pheromones in the air."

"I thought the distraction would be a good lesson. Teach you to fight through such things."

"Sure, only I'm not going to be fighting him in the tournament. I know who I'm fighting then, and I'm not attracted to any of them. This—" she gestured at Shreve "—fighting him won't teach me how to survive. No offense," she added curtly to Shreve, who just blinked at her with a bemused expression on his face.

Asher looked at Shreve and shrugged. "She's probably right. But I still think you could help."

"How?" he asked.

"You seem to know your weapons. You improved the whip. You brought the katana. From your observations, what do you think she can do to improve?"

Shreve crossed his arms and gazed at her. "She's having too much fun. She's a natural fighter. Strong desire and instinct, but she's obviously enjoying her training."

"What's wrong with that?" she countered.

"Only that you seem to forget that you're fighting for your life."

"I *will* be."

"No." His voice was forceful. "Your head is in the wrong place. Every time you come here to train, you must feel your mortality. Realize every second is a battle, one that you can lose. You're overconfident. Your real opponents will be fighting for their lives, too. Bones, tissue, breath, and blood. One mistake, and your life is over. It only takes a second."

She looked at the ground, letting his words sink deep inside her mind. It was embarrassing how right he was. She wanted to impress him, but she'd obviously fallen short. She determined to make up for that in the future. She took her lumps and nodded. "You're right... Thank you."

She looked back up into his eyes. A well of sorrow lived there. It hurt her to see it. The light of the dawn encroached on them. She shook herself.

"I have to get home... Will I see you tonight?"

"It's not a good idea, Sabra," Shreve said.

"That's not what I asked."

He smiled in a hopeless kind of way. "Probably."

Reluctantly, she turned and ran back to the Lair, her stomach sinking deeper with each stride. She wanted to stay there, with him. Her stride beat the ground as she ran. She pouted internally. Back to reality. Stupid, misogynistic, heartless reality.

CHAPTER TEN

Shreve watched Sabra run away until he couldn't see her anymore. Asher came up behind him and slapped him companionably on the back.

"She heard you. I can tell when she is really listening, and she was listening. Those were wise words. She needed them."

He turned and looked down at Asher.

He smiled at Shreve's tortured expression. "Sit down, son. We need to talk."

He ran his hands through his hair and sighed. "It will take a while."

"I'm sure it will."

They sat on blocks from a crumbled foundation, facing each other.

"I'm going to tell you everything, Asher. I only ask that you wait until I am finished before you pass judgment on me. It will be hard. Some of my story is going to anger you."

Asher crossed his ankles, laced his fingers over his stomach, and nodded. "Go on. I'll do my best to keep a cool head."

"I wasn't born in Regia. I wasn't born at all, actually. I was engineered by the wizards. I'm the clone of a monster, and for most of my life, I believed the monster to be my father. I followed him in whatever he did. He used me as an instrument of evil and pain. It was my life. I didn't know anything else...I'm going to show you my face, the face of my original, but before I do, I have to plead with you to remember this: I am *not* him! I disavow him."

This was probably the end, Shreve thought. He pushed ahead, taking a deep breath, and relaxing his face so his features slid back.

Asher scrambled to his feet, his eyes bugging.

"Copernicus," he wheezed.

Shreve instantly shifted his face back and held up his hands. "I am not him," he said again. "Remember what I said. Please! Remember how you decided to trust me. Your instinct, you said. I repent of my previous life. I renounced Copernicus before he died. That's how I got Forest's sword. I saved her life more than once. I rescued her from him."

Asher pulled a knife from his belt and thrust it against Shreve's neck. Shreve looked into his eyes. He made no move to defend himself.

"Go ahead, if you must. I understand. But you better cut really deep."

"Do you care nothing for your own life?" Asher demanded.

"I care more than I can express. I don't have much time left. My DNA is old, and I am beginning to deteriorate. Even if you don't kill me now, I will die soon...I'm trying to learn what is good and right. Trying to live it while I can. I'm trying to discover who I really am, so I might know myself before I die. Do you believe it is too late for me, Asher? I respect you. You *are* a good man. If you say there is no hope, then I will trust there is none, and I will feel grateful to you when you slit my throat."

Asher blinked and slowly pulled his knife back. He sat back down and put his head in his hands. "You're still alive. So there's hope." He blew out a heavy breath. "Of all the blasted things on the face of Regia that I've encountered in my long life, you take the cake."

Shreve's vision blurred with tears as hope surged in his heart. "Will you help me? Show me how to be a good man?"

He sighed again and nodded. "As best as I can. Tell me the rest. Tell me everything."

Shreve told him all about his life. They talked long into the afternoon. Asher's demeanor grew easier with him over the hours until Sabra finally entered their conversation.

"You said you owed her a debt. What did you mean by that?"

"I was there when her sister died. I saw it happen, and I didn't stop it. In truth, it was the moment that pushed me over the edge and made me decide to leave Copernicus. I was left alone to clean up and take care of the body, then Sabra came..." Emotion choked him, and he couldn't continue for a moment. "I had to watch her grief. I had to listen to her heart break."

"Did she see you?"

"Yes. We spoke briefly."

"Damn, Shreve. And now you love her."

"I do?"

"What do you think all that torture is you said you felt?"

"Oh..." he said, slowly. "I don't know anything about that...I don't know how..."

"Well, maybe you're not quite there yet. You obviously care about her, and you two have plenty of chemistry. Hell, I could've sworn I saw heat waves coming off the pair of you earlier today. Love is not that far of a leap from where you are."

"It's a bad idea."

Asher barked out a laugh. "Love is always a bad idea, except it's not an idea at all."

"What do I do?"

"You've got to tell her the truth of who you are. What you feel for her and what she feels for you cannot stand on a lie."

"What does she feel for me?"

"That I don't know beyond what she admitted today. She's attracted to you; you shared a connection in wolf form. You'll have to get the rest from her, but there's more in your way than your identity, how she's going to respond to it, and the fact that you're dying."

"There's more than that?"

105

"Yeah, there's Gahu. Her betrothed."

Shreve saw red, and his eyes burned. It was like his insides spontaneously combusted. He was instantly on his feet.

"Whoa, calm down there. It's arranged, not a love match. And she's indifferent to him, so much, in fact, that he plans to fight in the tournament, and she still plans to go ahead and fight, too."

Shreve took a deep breath and then another. The fire inside him didn't go out, but his eyes cleared. He was mollified slightly that Asher said she didn't love the guy. "I don't understand this tournament. Explain it."

Asher told him about it and the reasons she was fighting, to change things for the she-wolves. He told him about their culture, and that he agreed with Sabra about what was wrong with it.

"That's why I decided to train her. And that's why it has to be in private."

Shreve paced, agitated. "The whole thing is so stupid. Physical fighting, who's the strongest gets to be the leader. Why would anyone believe the biggest muscles equate to leadership skills? Sabra should be the leader. She has a *strong* heart, and *strong* ideas. Who cares if she's female?"

"Most of them do. No one else will support her. Well, none of the men, at least. As soon as she proclaimed she was going to fight, her brother rushed to arrange her with Gahu. And Gahu is a fool. He's not the worst choice, and he's a strong soldier, but he wants to hold her down, crush her spirit."

"Don't tell me anything else about him. Evil rises in me. I already want to kill him. I don't know how much self-control I have."

Instead of recoiling away from him and his pronouncement of murderous intention, Asher chuckled. "Yeah, you're not too far away from loving her…I can see you're confused. That's actually a very natural reaction."

"It is?" Shreve was shocked.

"I remember when I was first in love. If anyone would have told me some other guy had claimed my girl and was trying to stomp everything I loved about her, damn straight, I'd want blood."

"Interesting," Shreve said thoughtfully. "Again, I don't trust myself. So don't tell me any more about him."

"Sure. No problem."

"Does she have a real chance in the tournament? You know her competition."

"I think she has a chance—you've helped with that."

"I need to see them, watch them. Tell me their names."

Asher frowned. "How are you going to watch them?"

"I can do more than just shift. I can mimic real individuals, even females. I could hide in plain sight. You could show me where to go and who to impersonate."

"You've got to prove that to me. I need to see it."

Shreve shifted into a perfect likeness of Asher.

The old wolf threw his head back and guffawed loudly. "Okay. I'm sold. I'll take you in and direct you. But you cannot engage with these people. Agreed?"

Shreve shifted back. "Agreed. I'll follow your full advice. Of course, I don't need to go this way at all. It's a better idea for me to just go invisible. I'll just shadow you."

"Maybe a better idea *this* time. Give you the lay of things and a feel of the people. But this has to be quick. Some will be able to sense the presence of an elf. A shifter would blend better because our chemical makeup is so similar to theirs."

"Don't worry. If things get dicey, I can just open a portal and escape. Course I'm trying not to travel like that. It seems to put undue strain on my heart."

Asher pursed his lips. "You asked me to help you become a good man. Here's my first bit of advice. You are unlimited in your abilities. You can go anywhere and be anything. It might be hard, but respect others limitations. Most importantly, respect their boundaries."

"Clarify, please."

"Just because you can, doesn't mean you should. You could slip undetected into Sabra's bedroom, for example. Don't."

Shreve smiled obscenely wide.

"I'm going to shut up now, before I give you any more bad ideas," Asher said, wagging his finger at him. "Seriously, don't do that."

He continued to smile. "I won't, unless she asks me to."

Asher grunted. "Ready?"

"Lead on," Shreve said, his appearance fading into nothing.

Asher walked at a natural pace while he followed, taking in everything he saw and heard. Small ramshackle homes littered the outlying areas. It was clear these were the lower class. The whole area looked depressed. Despite their obvious poverty, the children played happily and loud. Shreve found himself unconsciously smiling. He would have enjoyed just standing and watching them. They were adorable and bursting with life and joy.

He wished each one of them well in his heart as he passed them. They were too young to know how blessed they were. That they were born, had families, and prospects. He envied them.

Asher led him to what looked like the main gathering place. People milled around, talking. He noticed immediately that the women and men were segregated. Anger sparked in him as they passed a couple of women. As soon as they saw Asher walking by, they all quieted and turned their eyes to the ground and hung their heads.

He imagined Sabra having to behave in such a way because the culture dictated it. He shook his head, disgusted. He couldn't think any more about that right now.

"I see Silhon and his gang of puppies up ahead. Pay attention to them. A few of them are fighting in the tournament," Asher said under his breath.

Shreve looked at the group of young men. He didn't need to be told which one was Silhon. Silhon swaggered like he was the emperor. His very pores oozed the arrogant stench of spoiled, inherited privilege. Nonetheless, he was fairly tall and muscled. Shreve didn't need to see him fight to gage his skill. In a fight against Sabra, not counting for situational circumstances but just on ability alone, she would win.

Then his eyes snapped onto one of the young men trailing behind Silhon. His blood ran cold at the sight of Gareth. Shreve grabbed Asher's arm.

"Is Gareth fighting in the tournament?" he whispered in Asher's ear.

Asher nodded his head in a quick little jerk. "How do you know him?"

"We need to talk about this. Let's go back to the shifter colony," Shreve said. "Quickly, please."

"What's the big deal?" Asher asked as soon as they were back and Shreve became visible again. "Gareth will be no challenge to Sabra. I've seen him spar before. He's sloppy, unskilled."

"You're wrong. That's a ruse. I know Gareth. He's hiding, quite effectively, behind that peacock, Silhon. Let me guess, after Copernicus died, he came home claiming he'd been forced into the Aluka Circle against his will?"

"Yeah. There were a few others besides him. No one likes to talk about that."

"The others probably were forced and turned into slaves, but not Gareth. Gareth came freely. And he's far from sloppy and unskilled. He was one of Copernicus' favorites. Copernicus had a team of the most vicious and deadly killers within the Circle. I've watched him in action... There's no way, no matter how good she might get, that Sabra can beat him. No way at all. Against him, she'll die very quickly."

"Shit. Well I guess that's that. She's going to have to drop out." He heaved a great sigh. "I don't know that she'll listen to me."

"She has to," Shreve said flatly. "There's no choice."

Asher shook his head. "I don't think it will make any difference to her. I truly think she'd rather die in the tournament than fall in line with the life Gahu has planned for her... You know how she is."

"I won't let her."

"Really?" he scoffed. "That's just the thing, Shreve. Just the attitude that makes her dig in her heels. A man ordering her about."

He took a moment to think about it. Asher was right. "I think you're going to have to talk to her about it. I...I'll mess it up. Just the thought of her up against Gareth makes me feel desperate, panicked."

Asher put his hand on his shoulder. "It'll be okay. Don't worry. There's still two and a half months before the tournament. A lot can happen in that time. We'll persuade her. I promise."

Shreve exhaled. "Okay. That's good. We'll figure it out in the time in between."

"Don't talk to her about this tonight."

"Why?"

"You've got to tell her who you are before you go any further in your relationship. Trust me. Get the truth out there and let the dust settle from it first."

"All right." He was dejected. "I'll trust your advice."

Asher left for home as the evening smeared across the sky like dancing brushstrokes. It was amazing to Shreve that he had a friend. He was learning quickly how strong the emotion and loyalty could be between friends. What he felt for Sabra was different, but there were elements that were the same.

He watched the moon climb up the sky and felt love for Regia, thankful that he would be able to die here and not in some other world.

He just had to hang on long enough to see Sabra through this hurtle in her life. He breathed deep, feeling the many pieces of his makeup. If only he was just one thing. If only he wasn't so fragmented. If only he had his own face. A face that belonged to no one but him. One that carried no judgment or fear. To live and just be.

He put his hands on his face and thought about Sabra. What did she see when she looked at him? What did he look like? It seemed as if his face rebuilt itself around her. A smile curved his lips. She obviously liked what she saw.

His stomach fluttered. She would be here soon, or probably. If she could get away. The soft, dreamy nature of his thoughts came down with a hard bump. He was going to lose her tonight, because he was going to tell her the truth. He surely didn't want to.

She didn't come running. She walked slowly, methodically. He watched her, his heart pulling tight. The moonlight slid through her hair, over her flawless skin, and glimmered in her purple eyes. There was something very different about her. He always saw her physically exerting herself, defiant energy bursting from her. But now, she was serene.

He would have moved toward her, but found he was momentarily frozen. She was a goddess, and she was out here to be with *him*. She spotted him, their eyes locking. A slow smile spread her perfect lips. He smiled back. A degree of heat flashed in her eyes. This was such a bad idea, worse than the nights before it.

What was going to happen? What did she want? What did she expect? He'd never been physically intimate with anyone. He'd never met anyone he wanted, until her. But he couldn't have her. Even though she wanted him back. He had to tell her the truth. She wouldn't want him after that. He sighed. *Those* fantasies would only ever be just fantasies.

She walked bravely up to him and stopped a mere foot away. "Shreve."

"Sabra." His throat was so dry.

She continued to smile. "Thank you for helping me today. I

appreciate your advice. I've thought about it a lot."

He *sort of* heard what she said. "You're gorgeous."

She blushed and looked down for a moment. "So are you," she whispered.

"What do you see when you look at me?"

"What do you mean?"

"What do I look like?"

She smirked. "Don't you know? Don't you have a mirror?"

"Not really. I have a shard from a broken mirror. I haven't looked at myself in a while."

She cocked her head to the side. "Where do you live?"

"In the Wolf's Wood. Next to the dryad graveyard. Would you like to see?"

"Yes." She held her hand out to him.

He looked down at it and clasped his hands behind his back. "I'm sorry. I can't touch you."

"Why?"

"Because I want to so much."

"That makes no sense."

He smiled sadly. "Doesn't it?"

She closed her eyes and took a deep breath. When she opened them again, the heat there hadn't banked, it surged. "It makes sense. You're denying nature. Why?"

"Asher told me about Gahu."

The desire in her eyes turned instantly into anger. "*I* didn't choose him!"

"I know that."

She turned and stomped a few paces away, then she turned on him again. "I don't know anything about you, except your name, and the way you make me feel. But I have this..." She pressed her hand under her sternum. "This...*certainty*."

"I have a certainty as well. I am certain that what I'm going to tell you tonight is going to turn whatever you feel for me into hatred."

She came toward him again. "Then don't tell me."

"I have to."

"No you don't. I probably won't win the tournament. But I will die trying. Because I refuse to live like this. As some man's property. But you, you're in my dreams. I watch the sun move over the sky, wishing it would hurry up, so I can come to you. I want you, whoever you are. We connected. I know you felt it, too. I think about how I don't have much time left and what time I do have, I want to spend with you."

It was too much. The force was too strong, and her words pulled him into a current he couldn't fight. He wrapped his arms around her. She tilted her head up and closed her eyes, her lips parting. He groaned as the pull took him under. He pressed his lips against hers. It was his first kiss. How could something so soft have such gravity? His mouth was closed, but hers was slightly open. Her lips pressed harder until he opened his mouth and took more. The second his tongue touched hers, she gasped and sucked the air from his lungs. She pulled at him, dragging him closer, until there was no space between them. It was over. He couldn't fight this. He was totally lost, going down in flames. Her hands gripped his shoulders tightly, still trying to pull him closer. Something exploded in his head, and he was desperate for more, for everything. He moved his mouth to her throat. He was going to eat her up. His hands ran over her body, greedy and fast.

"Slow down," she whispered. "I'm not going anywhere, and I want everything. I want all there is of you."

Slow down. Slow down. He repeated her words in his head. *Slow down... No. Stop. Stop now!* He had to tell her the truth. If he didn't, and things went further physically, and then she found out, she would hate him even more. And he'd deserve that. She had to know who she was with, otherwise, it just felt deceitful to him. Like he was stealing something.

His breath shuddered from his lungs. "You want all there is of me, except the truth."

She looked up at him. He saw the fire in her eyes lessen by degrees, replaced by confusion.

It was the very last thing he wanted to do, but he let go and took a step back from her. "Listen to me, Sabra. I never meant to interfere in your life. I never meant to see you again. That night, you ran past me…something changed in me when we ran together. I didn't know it would be like that."

"I felt your remorse that night," she said. "I didn't understand it. I still don't."

"Listen to my voice. You said you recognized my voice."

She shivered, and her eyes widened, then she shook her head. He groaned. This was the end, and he wasn't ready for it to be the end.

"Look at my face." He pushed his real face out.

Shock and horror flooded her wide eyes. "No." her voice was barely audible. *"No!"*

"I'm so sorry…for Sophie."

"Don't say her name, you bastard!" she shouted. "Don't ever say her name!"

She reared up and punched him in the face. His head snapped back, lights exploding behind his eyes. He exhaled raggedly and rotated his jaw.

"You've got a nerve putting your hands on me." She was practically vibrating with indignation.

"I'm sorry."

She turned on her heel, marched three steps, and stopped. She hung her head, and her shoulders slumped. Then she threw her head back, exhaling an odd kind of strangled cry. She looked back at him, her eyes fathomless. He felt his face shiver and shift back again to the face she naturally brought out of him. She turned all the way around and took two steps back toward him. He didn't move. He would take whatever pain and punishment she wanted to serve to him.

Color rushed into her cheeks. "This is so wrong... How could you? What have you done to me? You've got a nerve putting your hands on me," she repeated. Her whole body trembled. "Do it again," she whispered.

"What?"

She slapped him in the face. It stung and made his ears pop. But as he opened his eyes to look back at her, she grabbed him roughly around the back of the neck and pulled his head down, kissing him hard. Shock lasted only a second, then vanished behind violent lust. She kissed him so hot and so forcefully, until neither of them could breathe. His mind spun, and his body went into a rage equal to hers. She shuddered against him, but then she jerked her head back, and everything stopped as quickly as it had started.

Her lips were puffy and bruised. Her chin trembled. She looked long and direct into his eyes. "You were right." Her voice shook. "I hate you. Almost as much as I hate myself." She backed away. "Goodbye."

She turned and ran.

He fell to his knees. "*Sabra!*" His voice tore through the forest. The sound was fury, desire, anguish, and a plea all at once.

****

She stopped, panting, and braced her hand against a tree when she heard him call her name. Her heart clenched and rebelled. This wasn't happening. It wasn't the truth. And how? How had she just done that? How had she faced her enemy and still wanted him? Her traitorous body screamed and clawed, still on fire for him. She felt sick. Her stomach twisted. She pushed off again, running as fast as she could, all the way home. She didn't pay any mind to anything or anyone around her as she ran through the entrance of the mountain and up the stairs to her front door.

She burst into the living room, out of breath, surprising Gahu, who was sitting on the couch. She was horrified and jerked up short as he faced her. Shit! Why was he here now?! She felt exposed. How was she to cover the raging storm inside her and act normal?

"What are you doing here so late?"

"I was waiting for you. Where have you been at such an hour?" he demanded.

She took a steadying breath. "I was...I was running. I like running by myself at night."

He narrowed his eyes. "You were alone?"

"Of course. What's the problem?"

He surveyed her closely. She panicked. Could he sense her physical state? He walked to her and caught her up in his arms, pressing himself against her. *Gah, not this!* He was like acid on a burn.

"Your body's running hot, Sabra. Why is that? You're craving."

She pushed him back. "Don't embarrass me. It's not my fault...I...I was thinking about you." It felt like the most disgusting, dirtiest lie she'd ever told.

He smiled and grabbed her again, hauling her toward her bedroom. *Fine, whatever.* She thought. *This will end my insanity. It's what I deserve.*

He booted the door shut and bore down on her, kissing her mouth. She closed her eyes tight and tried to give in. He tasted wrong. He felt wrong. He moved wrong. She began shaking again, but it wasn't like the way she'd been with Shreve. Now she was shaking with revulsion.

"Don't be afraid," Gahu said. "Just trust me. I'll fulfill your desires."

Fat chance. Her shaking ratcheted up a notch. *I desire my enemy.*

He pulled at her clothes. This kind of substitution was a mistake, and she'd already more than filled her quota of mistakes for the day. She couldn't do this. It was a betrayal of herself. Rejection she couldn't fight against welled up inside her. Her stomach twisted again. "Wait. I'm not ready."

"You're more than ready." He pressed his hand on her abdomen under her navel where the fire burned hottest.

"Physically maybe, but I don't want to."

He ignored her protest and grabbed at the waist of her pants.

"I said no!"

"Stop it, Sabra. Relax. I'm going to ease your craving. I know it must hurt."

It did. It ached. But it was nothing to the pain in her heart. Her stomach churned harder. *No.* Everywhere he touched her cried out *no.* Something snapped inside her.

"Gahu?"

The deadly tone of her voice caught his attention. He looked into her face.

"I lied when I said I was thinking about you. I wasn't. I'm sorry. I can't be the woman you want. I'm never going to submit to you."

His cheeks flushed red, and his eyes flared. "We'll see about that, you're mine." He growled and tore her shirt open. "You're about to learn what that means."

She would have fought him off, but her vision clouded as he assaulted her. She saw Shreve, the way he looked waiting for her, the way he kissed her...who he really was. Her eyes focused back on Gahu. She was disgusted, distraught, and heartbroken. Her stomach pitched. Her body jerked forward, and she vomited on him.

His eyes bugged in shock, and he stepped back, his intentions of having a good time evaporated. He grimaced, seeing his shirt was covered with vomit.

"Wha... What's wrong with you? Are you sick?"

She wiped her mouth. "Apparently. You should leave."

He did. Quickly. Sabra fell into a momentary numbness as she cleaned herself, and the floor, and went to bed. She lay on her back, looking at the moonlight spilling into her room through the window. She hurt all over. She wasn't sick, at least not the way Gahu thought. Her body still ached for Shreve. She was too hot. She kicked her blanket off and stood. She leaned on the window's edge and took a deep breath of the cool night air. It brought no comfort. He was out there.

She turned away and laid back down, pressing her hands to her head. "Forgive me, Sophie, I didn't know. I never would have...I hate him. I know I promised I would avenge you, but I can't. I have no one to exact justice on for you. Only Shreve. And I can't..."

Her mind pulled deep into her memories of that night. Finding Sophie dead in the aftermath of revelry of the Aluka Circle. And there was Shreve with his other face. She could never forget what he'd said. She remembered everything about that moment with perfect clarity. She'd asked if he was Sophie's killer.

"No. But I didn't help her, either."

"You're one of them, aren't you? The Aluka circle?"

"Yes," he admitted.

"I am no one, yet. But someday, I will stop all of you. If the rest of Regia cannot stop you, then the wolves will. And I will lead them."

"Good luck to you then. My condolences on your loss. What is your name?"

"Sabra, and don't you forget it."

"I can assure you, I won't."

She groaned and rolled over onto her stomach, burying her face in her pillow. She believed him. She believed him then, and she believed him now. He didn't kill Sophie. She'd run with him, *twice*. They connected on that deep spiritual plane only wolves could. In that state,

118

she trusted him so much, she'd even fallen asleep next to him!

Still, the nerve of him! He'd known who she was all along. He'd played with her. Deceived her. Made a fool of her. It was unforgivable. Wasn't it?

What was he? She'd run with him. He was a wolf. But he shifted, too. The green eyes, the black hair, the face that made her throat dry with wanting—was that the real him? Or was it the other one? The face she knew in her nightmares, the face her hate was attached to? No matter, it was *his* face and just seeing it on him aimed and shot deep into her heart. A direct hit on her softest place with cruel, surgical accuracy.

Memories of her sister assailed her. "I will never see him again, Sophie. I promise."

Her ears rung with the phantom of his voice as he called her name, and she did something she'd sworn she never would again... She cried.

In the morning, Sabra locked herself in her room and didn't leave it for days.

CHAPTER ELEVEN

"I don't want to leave you." Syrus held her face in his hands.

"I'm all right."

"No, you're not." He ran his finger gently under her eye. "You're so tired."

Forest pressed her palm against his chest. "You'll know if something's wrong. Rahaxeris got back last night, he'll be over here soon. You need to go to work."

He leaned down and kissed her deeply. He put his hand over hers. "You know how to reach me."

Tesla bumped into their legs. Syrus smiled down at her and lifted her up. She clung around his neck. Her hands lit up. He rubbed them, and the energy quieted under his touch. He kissed her cheek.

"Be a good girl for mommy."

She nodded.

He set her down and kissed Forest again before leaving for work. After he left, Tesla stood by the front door, and began to cry.

"It's all right, sweetheart. He'll be back later."

She wasn't consoled. Forest picked her up, wincing as her daughter's hands stung and burned her. She began kicking and thrashing. Forest set her back down. She turned away and toddled to her room. Forest watched her retreat, a singular kind of pain spreading through her chest. This pain was new, but Forest was becoming increasingly familiar with it. It pleaded desperately and stretched out like an endless thread of desolation pulled right through her core. This pain wasn't sharp with peaks and valleys, it was constant without an end in sight. As it pulled through, it snagged and unraveled her.

She followed Tesla to her room. The doorframe was hard against her back as she sat on the floor and watched her daughter. Various toys lay scattered around. Since Tesla had aged, the reasons or patterns to her actions and play made no sense to Forest. She watched her, tried to analyze and understand, but since the incident with the flower, she knew Tesla didn't see the world the same way she did.

Forest tried to engage and play with her. Sometimes she hit on the right thing and Tesla would stick with her for a while, but those moments were few and far between. She longed so greatly, more than any desire she'd ever felt, for her daughter to know that she loved her. Hand in hand with that desire, was the longing that her child would love her in return. She thought it unnatural that she should have doubts on such things, yet they were there, like shadows in the corners.

"Would you like to listen to some music, Tesla?"

Tesla made no show that she had heard. Forest crossed to the other side of the room and turned on the stereo. Her little hands stopped stacking the blocks. She looked up, her eyes wide. Forest sat next to her as the classical flute music filled the room.

Forest smiled at her. "Music. Do you like it?"

Tesla blinked a few times. She covered her ears with her hands and then removed them, put them back, and removed them again. Her face relaxed, and she closed her eyes. Forest breathed a sigh of relief. She liked it.

After a few moments, the flutes and wind instruments were joined with the string section. Tesla's eyes flew open at the sound of the violins. She cringed inward, her hands now pressing hard against her ears, and screamed at the top of her lungs.

Forest jumped up and turned off the music. When she turned back around, Tesla was on the other side of the room, banging her head against the wall.

Panicked, Forest rushed to her, grabbing her by the shoulders. Tesla strained against her mother's grip and hit her head once more.

Forest pulled her away from the wall while she kicked and flailed.

"Stop!" Forest begged her. "Stop!"

She held her close, sinking to the floor, cross-legged. Tesla turned on her and sank her fangs into Forest's forearm. She yelled in pain and shock as her child attacked her, biting her repeatedly and burning her with her hands.

Forest's consciousness sank back, as if it crouched in a dark crevice of a tunnel. She held still, her eyes going hollow, as her heart wailed from that desolate place. Her baby, her sweet baby, who she loved more than her own life, who she would do anything for, was hurting her on purpose.

Then Syrus was there. He lifted Tesla off Forest. She didn't see what he did to calm her. She left the room, moving through the house and out into the garden. She sat on the bench next to the fountain and collapsed into bitter tears. *Why? Why? Why?* Her heart cried.

She leaned all the way over and looked at the ground. For a long time, she just stared at a rock in the dirt next to her foot. *I can't go on like this...but I have no choice. I can't, but I have to. I don't want this to be my reality... What I want is irrelevant.*

A hand rubbed her back. "Forest?"

She sat up, wiping her nose and leaned her head against Rahaxeris' sharp shoulder. "Dad. I'm so glad you're back. I need your help."

"What's wrong?"

She wiped the tears away and sighed. "You've got to examine Tesla. She's not the baby you left. She's a toddler. She aged about two years in a few minutes in an electrical storm, or something like that. She can't talk. She tries, really hard, you can see her straining, but just these weird noises come out. And the other day, she took a picked flower and turned it into a machine."

"*What?*"

"That's what Syrus said. He calls it an organic machine. The flower blooms, withers, dies, and then starts over and blooms again. I'll show you, but please, please help her."

"I will do everything I can. There's some tests I can run on her. It won't hurt her, don't worry."

Forest exhaled heavily and smiled. "I know you wouldn't hurt her."

He stood, held out his hands, and pulled her to her feet. Worry creased his brow as he looked at her straight on. "You're exhausted. You should go lay down for a while. I assume Syrus is inside?"

"Yeah, he's here."

"Good. You go take a nap. We can handle Tesla."

She hugged him. "Thanks, Dad."

****

Rahaxeris watched from the doorway of the nursery, keeping his exterior cool and collected while his mind reeled seeing his granddaughter. Syrus looked at him from the rocking chair, Tesla in his lap.

"Where is Forest?"

"She's lying down."

Rahaxeris came into the room. Tesla looked at him and smiled. She wiggled to get down. He leaned over as she came to him, wrapping her arms around his neck.

"Hello, my pretty girl. I missed you. Did you miss me?"

She nodded.

"You've grown a whole bunch since I left. A little too much, I'd say."

The child looked directly into his eyes, unflinching and pointed. He raised his eyebrows. She was certainly trying to convey something without words. Her pupils dilated, opening like a door, beckoning him to come in. There was a level of consciousness far beyond that of a normal two-year-old behind her grey eyes. It was as if she was trying to force him to understand. He caught something of it.

"You're in a hurry to get older?"

She nodded again.

"You made it happen?"

She smiled.

"I need to see this flower Forest mentioned."

Syrus left the room for a second, and then returned, the flower in his hand. Rahaxeris shifted Tesla to his hip and looked down at it. He watched it go through one whole life cycle, a deep frown on his face.

Rahaxeris looked at Syrus. "I need to take her to Kyhael, if it's all right with you. Forest's already agreed that I can test her. I don't want to disturb her again if she's asleep."

"I'm coming with you. I'll stay out of your way, or I'll help, whatever you need. I'll just leave Forest a note in case she wakes."

"Good." Rahaxeris smiled at Tesla. "Let's go play at Grandpa's workshop."

He opened a portal for them straight into *Rune-dy* headquarters. As soon as the portal closed, Tesla went rigid in Rahaxeris' arms. Her eyes widened, and her hair stood on end. She seemed caught in a state of apprehension.

Rahaxeris set her on her feet. For a moment, she didn't budge an inch. Then very slowly, she began to look around the main room.

"What now?" Syrus asked.

"Let's just watch what she does first. See what interests her. This place holds so many forces and magic. What is going to attract or repel her?"

"She's moving so slowly."

"I think she can perceive things we cannot."

Tesla walked over to one side of the room, looking intently at the floor. She touched the Bellis stone with one fingertip. A snake of red electricity absorbed into the pores of the stone from her finger. A flicker, then the transparent image of Hezeron appeared on the floor, where he'd died. Hezeron didn't resemble a ghost, but a molecular map of his biometrics in red light. Another flicker, and he grew more transparent layers like a Da Vinci anatomy sketch.

Tesla pulled her finger back from the floor, and the image of Hezeron vanished. She looked up at her father and grandfather watching. She curled her hands and winced. She held her hands out to Rahaxeris, beginning to cry out in pain. The red crisscrossed on her hands, the light throbbing in time with her pulse.

He took her hands and pulled the excess magic from her. She quieted.

Tesla moved about the space more freely. She touched the walls as she walked. Momentary images sprang out of the walls everywhere she touched. When she came to the open door of the laboratory where Menjel used to operate, experiment, and torture, she cringed away from it and began shaking.

Rahaxeris closed the door. What could she see? What did she feel in that horrid room? Rahaxeris felt a chill every time he went in there, but nothing else. He could dig deeper into the spiritual level in there, but he chose not to. He'd witnessed the evil committed there in real time, in flesh and blood.

She moved on down the hall and took a turn toward Rahaxeris' personal quarters. She pointed up at the beam of light coming through the wall. He lifted her up so she could touch it. She smiled as the light began to grow. The three of them went through the light into the room beyond.

Very few people had ever been in here. Rahaxeris was slightly self-conscious. His memories were stored in the stone walls. Tesla would obviously have no trouble accessing them. That prospect was not acceptable to him. Maybe she wouldn't comprehend the adult nature of his memories, but he wasn't all right with his son-in-law seeing them. Just a bit too awkward and inappropriate.

He was about to suggest they go look at another space, when Tesla zeroed in on a very particular place on the wall. Rahaxeris was both frightened and amazed. She walked straight to the place he'd hidden the tesseract. Like the light beam, it was too high for her to reach. Again she pointed at the seemingly blank space of rock wall.

He shook his head. "That's not for you, sweetheart."

Her cheeks flushed in what was obvious temper and pointed again.

"No. I'm sorry. You can't have that."

"What is she pointing at?" Syrus asked.

Before he could answer, a terrible cracking noise split the air. Tesla's hands lit up. Orbs of energy stretched out over her hands like ball lightning. She placed both of her hands over her heart. The whole room was engulfed in an electrical storm. Her little body lifted off the ground. A red lightning wall held them away from her. Syrus grabbed the electricity in his hand, twisted, and pulled it down.

Another deafening crack sounded as the storm fizzled out, leaving behind thick smoke. Tesla crashed to the floor, unconscious.

Syrus lifted her up and held her. He looked desperately at Rahaxeris. "How do we stop this?"

Rahaxeris gazed at his now six-year-old granddaughter. "I don't think we can. She knew what she was doing. She did it to herself."

"You don't know that!"

"I know what I—"

Tesla coughed and opened her eyes. She pushed against her father's hold and stood up, smiling smugly and triumphantly at them.

Rahaxeris touched the top of the opposite wall, its surface rippling and turning reflective like a mirror. She walked over to it and looked at herself, running her fingers through her now waist-long hair. Her clothes were tattered and scorched from her transformation. Rahaxeris dug into his closet and gave her one of his shirts. She pulled it over her head. The tunic looked like a shapeless knee-length dress on her.

She looked at them and opened her mouth, but again only strange, strangled noises came out. She strained and coughed, growing upset. Her attention settled on her father. Silent tears ran slowly down his face. Her emotions changed at the sight of his. She went to him, her face crumpling as though she too were going to cry. He picked her up. She touched his face and shook her head, a small hum coming from her throat. She smiled and rested her forehead against his.

"She's trying to comfort you."

Syrus sighed, trying to let go of everything he felt at that moment. It was all just too overwhelming.

Tesla looked back at her grandfather and again, she pointed at the wall.

"Okay, Tesla," Rahaxeris said. "Hold on. I understand you want the cube. But it's too important. I can't let you have it."

She bared her teeth at him. He raised his eyebrows in surprise and exchanged a look with Syrus. "She certainly has a temper."

Syrus smirked. "She gets that from her mother... We have to help her communicate."

Rahaxeris drummed his finger against his lips. "I need to give her a physical examination. Let's go to my lab."

Tesla sat still on the table in the center of the sterile room while her grandfather poked and prodded at her. He focused predominately on her hands, the red light flower shape around her heart, and her throat. She cried out when he drew a small amount of her blood, but she submitted to it once he explained why he needed to jab her with a needle.

He put her blood under his scope. On the cellular level, the effects and damage of the Malachi Serum she'd received in utero were obvious. Despite the fact that she was chronologically only five months old,

Tesla's blood reflected her uncanny aging. It was, indeed, the blood of a six-year-old.

He put her through a series of cognitive tests. Her intelligence was off the charts. It unnerved him. *She* unnerved him. Her desire to get the cube unnerved him most of all. How did she know it was there? Why did she want it?

Syrus waited in the corner of the room, his back against the wall, watching the whole thing intently. His stress showed all over his body language and hung heavy in his eyes.

Rahaxeris gave her a book on sign language to look at. She eagerly put her nose in it, her eyes racing over the pages.

"So?" Syrus asked.

"There's nothing wrong with her throat, or her vocal chords. She's a genius. But unfortunately, there's a disconnect or disruption in her brain that prevents her from forming words aloud. That doesn't mean she doesn't think clearly what she wants to say. She should be able to communicate through sign language and writing. Perhaps, one day she might be able to speak, who knows... She's healthy, aside from the obvious."

He looked over at his daughter. "Is she *really* reading?"

"I would say so."

"But she hasn't been taught."

Rahaxeris shrugged. "She didn't need to be taught, she's hyperlexic. She just knows."

Syrus rubbed his hands over his face. "This is unbelievable," he said more to himself.

"Remember," Rahaxeris warned. "There's nothing wrong with her hearing. Just because she might be silent, doesn't mean she doesn't understand. Be careful what you say."

He exhaled raggedly. "Forest is going to take this really hard."

Rahaxeris clapped him bracingly on the shoulder. "We have to do all we can to help her through this."

Syrus nodded, and he focused his eyes back on Tesla. "What was she trying to get in your room?"

"The key to protecting Regia from the wizards."

Rahaxeris was anxious when they took Tesla home. Concerned how Forest was going to cope with her child now being six, a genius, and a mute. He kept Tesla out in the garden while Syrus went into the house to talk to her.

Tesla sat on the bench next to him, still reading the sign language book. She set it down and began to practice. His heart plummeted instantly as he saw a complication he'd not yet considered. The magic had pooled in her hands again, causing too much pain for her to sign well. She made a frustrated sound and clenched her hands. Then she stretched her fingers out and tried again. Her hands and forearms shook with the effort as she formed a few basic movements.

She held her hands out to him. He pulled the excess out, easing the pain. She sighed and tried again.

Grandpa, she spelled out.

"Good!" he exclaimed, smiling.

She pointed at the house and signed, *Mom, Dad*.

He nodded and even though he didn't need to, he signed, *I love you, Tesla. Your mom and dad love you. You're special. They are confused. They need time to learn how to be your parents. You must be patient with them.*

She nodded. *What did you think of the flower?*

"I was impressed. How did you do that?"

Can't explain. You wouldn't understand.

"Do you think your father understands?"

A little. His power, my power. Same. Mine goes deeper. She looked at him speculatively. *Your power is great. Sharp. I like your place. So much there.*

"You mean in Kyhael?"

Yes. Can I go back soon? Just you and me? Want to show you things I can do. Don't like the sad way Dad looks at me. Don't want to scare him.

"Maybe tomorrow. I'll ask your mom."

She looked back at the house and flexed her hands, they were getting fatigued and achy.

They are sad I am not still a baby.

"Yes," he admitted. "I am, too."

Too many things to do. Danger comes. Baby hands, clumsy.

The front door opened. Forest and Syrus stood on the threshold. He had his arm wrapped supportively around her. Her face was white as she looked at Tesla, and she quickly dashed a tear off her cheek. She rallied immediately and smiled at her daughter.

Tesla looked back up at Rahaxeris. He smiled and patted her shoulder. "Be kind to your mother. She needs tenderness from you, just as you need it from her. Remember, have patience with them. They're learning. I'll come see you again tomorrow."

She nodded, picked up the sign language book, and walked into the house. Rahaxeris sighed and left with a heavy heart. It had been a most unusual afternoon, giving him an abundance of things to ponder. He sent himself to the Onyx Castle to talk to Merhl and set a meeting time with everyone working on the wizard problem. Now that he had the cube, the time had come to form a real plan. He thought about Tesla, would she be a part of the solution?

CHAPTER TWELVE

There was no substance to the world. It flattened out like a picture. A representation of something real, but nothing more. Shreve wanted to go numb. He'd been numb plenty in his life. The harder he desired it, the more acute his feelings became. He was a three-dimensional being walking through a two-dimensional world. Was there even still a point to the remains of his life? Sabra hated him. Was it possible to still help her without her knowing it?

He walked slowly, directionless, looking at the moon where it peeked through the branches of the trees. It had been four days. She hadn't come back. And she wouldn't. Four days of bitter desolation, remembering the sweet impossible in the days before. She wouldn't come back, he told himself again. There was no sense to the hope that still lived inside him. The hope was a relentless sting, and he began to consider it his most formidable enemy. He longed for it to die.

He crossed his arms and continued walking. He was still in the Wolf's Wood. The hope pushed him to venture out back to where Sabra had come to him before. He fought against the urge.

A twig broke to his left.

His eyes snapped up and onto a familiar face.

"You!" Redge yelled. Shock, fear, and rage all traveled over his features in one second.

Sword drawn, he charged at Shreve. Shreve didn't have the energy to care. He faced Redge, his hands open. He remembered Redge well. He was no fool, and because of that, he struck while he could. Shreve didn't fault him as his broad sword slid straight into his core.

Blood rose up Shreve's throat, and the usual pain of such a wound shivered out and through his body. Shreve grabbed Redge's shoulder and pushed him backward. He sighed as the sword left his body. His wizard blood instantly began rebuilding his torn flesh.

Redge swung his sword, this time at his neck. He didn't flinch. The blade stopped short, giving the side of his neck a little nick.

"Don't move, Shreve," Redge ordered.

Shreve held his hands up again. "Sure. I'm not going anywhere. By the way, a strike to my torso isn't going to be enough to kill me. If you decide you're going to finish me, after all, you'd better cut off my head."

Redge narrowed his eyes. "You ran away? Copernicus thought you were dead."

"I had enough. It wasn't my fight. I didn't believe in it. Copernicus was insane."

"But he was your father."

"No. The only father I can claim is Rahaxeris. And that claim is a bit weak...Copernicus was created by Rahaxeris. I'm a clone, created by the wizards."

Redge's expression hardened. "I've seen who you are, what you're capable of. I should kill you right now."

"Go ahead." His voice was blasé. "There's no doubt I deserve it."

"No doubt," Redge reiterated fiercely.

"What's going on?" A woman came up behind Redge.

"Stay back, Journey," Redge ordered.

She didn't listen and continued forward. She had jeweled pink eyes that stood out strikingly against her dark skin. She aimed her gaze at Shreve's chest and began to hum a low note deep in her throat.

He was frozen in place as her voice went straight into his heart, hooked it, and pulled it right out of him. His vision trembled. Memories so deep, forgotten long ago, rose up through his consciousness like ship wreckage from the ocean floor brought to the surface. He fell hard into her song, unaware of time or his surroundings. He floated.

When he slowly came back to the present, he found himself sitting on the ground, his back against a tree, with the sounds of arguing in his ears. He listened, but gave no sign he was awake.

"His heart is pure."

"That's not possible, Journey. You just see the good in people and ignore the bad."

"Like the bad in you, right?" she countered.

"He's done—"

"I know what he's done, way more than you do. I've read his heart. And yes, he did terrible things. Unforgivable things."

"Good. I'm glad you can see that."

"Just like you. *You* kidnapped your best friend's life mate and almost beat her to death while she was pregnant."

Redge swore a few times. "Why would you throw that in my face? I was under a slave mark!"

"That's right." Her voice took a softer tone. "Now relax and shut up for a moment while I teach you something."

He didn't reply.

"You should have compassion for him. He was raised in a more cruel and brutal way than either of us could fathom. From his very beginnings, he was taught evil, to love it, to create it. That wasn't his fault. He was a child... Yes, he was good at what he was taught, unfortunately for many, but for him also."

"So you're saying he shouldn't be held accountable for his crimes?" Redge challenged.

"I'm not saying that. That's not my arena. Hailemarris is Forest's job. What I *am* saying is he deserves a chance. He wants to do the right things. He's striving for it. Miraculously, there is good in him. If it weren't for his goodness, you never would have been forgiven. If it weren't for him, Forest and Tesla would have died. Just think about that. You would have carried that for the rest of your life, and you would have lost your best friend, irrevocably."

"He's dangerous."

"He didn't attack you when you put your sword through him a few minutes ago. He could have killed you easily."

"Easily?" He was offended.

"He's part wizard...yes, easily."

Redge huffed and was quiet for a moment. "I'd say let's take him to Forest, but Syrus would kill me for bringing a criminal around his family. Since he could defeat me so easily, as you claim. How can we contain him?"

"I don't think we need to. Just ask him to come with us."

"I don't know about this, Journey. I don't, I *can't* trust him... Your skills put him under hard. He hasn't surfaced yet. I could just kill him now and be done with it."

"I know you don't really mean that. It's just your worry talking... Trust me. He's not a threat. Besides, he's totally lovesick."

"What?"

"Yes. He's completely gone over a she-wolf."

"You know, this is why I never liked you reading my heart. You find things a guy never wants found."

She laughed. "Men bury the most important things and deny they feel them, which leads to stupidity at crucial moments."

Shreve could feel their eyes on him and decided it was a good time to *wake up*. He lifted his head and met their gazes.

"So." He stood and dusted off his backside. "Where are we going?"

Redge looked at Journey. She smiled. He pulled out a phone, keeping his eyes trained on Shreve, and put it to his ear.

"Yeah, it's me. Where are you?" he said into the phone. "Okay, I've got, *found* Shreve… Yup, he's alive. No, he's not resisting, not yet anyway. We're near the Heart. Are you--"

Redge was cut off as a black gash tore the air open next to him. He and Journey stepped back from the portal as Rahaxeris came striding out of it. His red eyes fastened instantly on Shreve. Shreve held still, not sure what was about to happen. Then, unexpectedly, Rahaxeris smiled. He strode forward and embraced Shreve tightly.

His heart ached at the surprising show of affection. Rahaxeris was happy to see him. The idea that anyone could be happy to see him was foreign, but it brought nourishment to his emaciated soul. He released him abruptly.

"I'm glad you're still alive, Shreve. Where have you been?"

"Keeping to myself, mostly. Trying to make amends. Not very successfully, I'm afraid."

"Well, I think I know someone who would like to see you."

"Who?" Shreve was bewildered.

"Forest."

"Oh…are you sure? I mean, she'll remember the part I played in…I have *his* face."

"Don't you want to meet your niece?" Rahaxeris pressed.

Shreve half panicked. "I…I would love to, but I have no right to be around her. It is enough for me to know she is alive… She's not really my niece anyway."

Rahaxeris' red eyes bore down severely on Shreve. "Listen to me. You are a part of a family. Unconventional, sure, but a family nonetheless. You have me, Forest, and now Tesla."

He exhaled slowly, overwhelmed, and shook his head. "*Your* family. *Syrus'* family. Not mine. I'm sure Syrus would never agree to my presence. I wouldn't, if I were him."

A small smile curved the side of Rahaxeris' sharp mouth. "Don't underestimate my son-in-law."

"Oh, I'm not. Trust me... As much as I would love to come with you to see them, I just can't. It's not right."

"You think they'd be afraid of you." It wasn't a question. "Sorry to bruise your ego, but you're not that scary. Forest killed Copernicus while she was pregnant. Cut his head open like a cabbage. And I could kill you right now, without breaking a sweat."

Shreve smiled easily. He looked over at Redge and Journey and then back at Rahaxeris. "All right. But if things go south, it's entirely your fault."

"Fair enough. I'll take the blame. Let's go." He looked over at Redge and Journey. "Thank you for *detaining* him. I need the both of you at Kyhael tomorrow morning."

He opened another portal, and he and Shreve went through it together. They landed in Forest's garden. Memories assailed Shreve, and he found he couldn't move. This was the exact place he'd brought Forest, a breath from death, not knowing if he was in time, or if anyone could save her from the poison in her body. It was amazing to him that Syrus had been up to the task.

"I really doubt this is a good idea," he reiterated.

"Just wait here. I'm sure it's *not* a good idea to surprise them. Give me a minute. I'll be right back."

Shreve contemplated bolting as soon as the front door closed behind Rahaxeris. This was folly. He looked at the charming stone house, the light was warm in the windows against the darkening night. The place had something. A feeling. Simple comfort. They could live in the finest place in Regia, and they chose to live here.

After a few minutes, it wasn't Rahaxeris who came out. It was Syrus. He approached methodically, his eyes were flashing, and red electric currents snaked over his hands and forearms. His warning display of power was perfectly controlled. Shreve held his hands out, palms up, in a show of surrender.

"I know this is vulgar. I… It wasn't my idea. I'll leave."

"Wait," Syrus ordered.

They regarded each other silently for a moment. Shreve couldn't read Syrus. He didn't understand.

"Why did you save Forest?"

"I had to… She… She's my sister. I only wish I would have brought her to you sooner than I did. She was hurt by the poison, wasn't she?"

"Yes, and the baby."

A terrible pain built behind Shreve's eyes. "I'm sorry. I wish I had other words than that. I think it best if I leave now. This is your family. I would never do anything to hurt them, or you. I'm glad my sister has a man like you to protect her."

"Rahaxeris has vouched for you. Your actions have spoken for you. I owe you more than I could ever repay, for bringing Forest back to me. But I'll admit it's hard to look at you and not strike. You look just like him. It puts me on edge. And how do I know you're not going to go crazy like him any moment?"

"Fair point. I don't know that myself. It's safer if I leave." He turned and began walking away.

"Stop, Shreve." Syrus' voice was softer than it had been a moment ago.

He turned around and found himself face-to-face with Forest. So vibrant and full of life. Her riot of bronze hair burned in the darkness around her beautiful open face. The layered depth of her green eyes shimmered with feeling. She reached out and hugged him. He was frozen in shock for a second, then he wrapped his arms around her. His heart expanded. She was more of a stranger than anything, and yet… She belonged to him. As if the DNA they shared recognized itself in the other. Her shoulders began shaking with tears. He held her protectively, experiencing new and fierce emotions. He didn't understand what he felt, or what it was even called… *Storge*, family love. Everything felt so odd and off inside him. Too pleasant; it couldn't be real.

She pulled away and wiped at her eyes. "Sorry. I didn't mean to cry on you. I'm a little emotional these days."

"That's okay." He smiled.

Shreve looked around and found that Syrus had gone, giving them some privacy.

"Thank you for coming. Dad said you were hesitant."

"I was. Am...was."

"Thank you for saving my baby's life, and mine."

"I'm sorry about all the rest of it. I'm not making excuses, but I wasn't walking my own path. I was just following."

She tilted her head, looking closely at him. "You're special. You look like Copernicus, but not at the same time. You're different. You are your own person."

"You're very kind. I'm trying to be my own person. I'm searching for myself."

"What have you found so far?"

He blew out a breath and thought about it. "I hate lies. I can't make myself tell them anymore. Even at moments where I'd rather not say things, I can't lie. I wish I was just one thing. One race. I wish I had my own face, sometimes I feel like I do, when I'm with..."

She raised her eyebrows and smiled. "When you're with whom?" she prompted.

He blushed. "Never mind. It's over anyway, because I couldn't lie. She wants nothing to do with me now that she knows who I am. I don't blame her, I just miss her."

"I'm sorry."

"It's certainly not your fault," he said.

"I'm sorry you're hurting over her, whoever she is."

"Thank you."

"Are you ready to come inside? Meet Tesla? Have dinner with us?"

He looked longingly at the house. "That's a very generous offer. Maybe too generous."

"I'm asking for your company. Are you really going to deny me?"

He looked into her eyes and caved. "I can't when you ask like that."

She hooked her arm through his and pulled him toward the front door. The ease in the way she touched him planted the seed of something deep in his heart. Forest showed him mercy. Of all people, he didn't deserve anything from her, and yet she gave.

She stopped on the threshold. "I should warn you about Tesla. She's aging in an odd and accelerated way. She's only five months, but you'll find her a six-year-old. She has Syrus' power, and her hands can give you a nasty shock." Everything about Forest sagged. "She's also a mute. She can use sign language, but her hands hurt her so much, it's just a small amount of time that she can communicate...I just wanted you to be prepared. She understands everything said."

"She sounds amazing. I can't wait to see her. I'm sure she's beautiful."

Forest smiled at that. "Why are you sure of that?"

"Because you're her mother."

She raised one eyebrow. "You're charming, Shreve. Add that to your list of things you know about yourself."

He walked into the house, instantly enveloped in the warmth. Home. He'd never been in a place where that word, or idea, made sense until that moment. This was a real home. Forest towed him to the couch and gave him a small shove, forcing him to sit. At that moment, he realized what had just happened, and his heart leapt. When she shoved him, Forest had claimed him as her brother.

She sat next to him. Syrus and Rahaxeris were talking in the next room. His stomach growled at the aroma coming from the kitchen. He looked around at everything, unsure what to say, when Tesla came out of the other room. She walked directly up to him.

Shreve was dumbfounded by the girl. She was insanely beautiful, with an otherworldliness about her. He felt trapped under her unblinking, pewter gaze. It was as though she had witch eyes. The wizard in him realized she wasn't just looking at him, or taking his measure. She could see the layers of things others didn't even know existed. She dissected him.

Forest squirmed. "Tesla, this is—"

Shreve held his hand up to silence Forest without breaking eye contact with Tesla. "Let her finish," he said quietly.

She continued to stare for another thirty seconds, then, finally, she blinked and took a seat in the chair opposite the couch. She looked over at her mother, extending her fingers. Now that she had released his gaze, he looked at her hands. They were marvelous, brilliant, but he could see the effects of the pressure inside them. He imagined the pain was excruciating. It made him hurt knowing that she hurt. He wished he could take the pain from her.

Her hands trembled as she tried to sign something. The movements were jerky. She gave up, rubbing her hands together. He crooked his finger at her. She jumped down and walked back over to him. He held his hands out for hers.

"Oh, no, Shreve." Forest protested. "She'll hurt you."

He smiled. "Well, so it's an experiment. Give me your hands, Tesla."

She put her hands in his. The energy didn't slide into him, it rammed. It didn't hurt as he assumed it would. It was more of a rush, like a cold wind in his veins, pushing into his cells and marrow. He rubbed her fingers, and she smiled brightly at him. The child's smile slew him. He'd give her anything she wanted. She owned him.

"Oh, come on!" Forest complained. "You can do it, too?"

Shreve looked at her. "Do what?"

"You can ease her pain. Syrus can, and Dad, too. But I can't! It's not fair."

Tesla looked at her mom. *Maybe it's because you're a girl.* She signed.

Forest smirked. "We'll have to test that theory with the next guy you meet."

He's my uncle?

"That's right," Forest said.

Shreve didn't understand the signs.

He's really messed up, Mommy. He's dying.

A bad look came over Forest's face. "Are you sure?"

Tesla nodded. Forest looked at him, with that terrible expression.

"What?" he asked. "What did she say?"

"She said you're dying."

"Oh...that. Yeah. She's right. I am."

A long awkward silence followed his statement.

"How?" Forest asked finally.

He shrugged. "Just a side effect of being a clone. Old DNA doesn't make a long-standing foundation."

"I'm sorry." She truly sounded it. "Do you know how long you have?"

"No."

"Do you know?" she asked Tesla.

Tesla looked closely at his chest, squinting her large eyes. He had the sneaky suspicion she was examining the inside of his heart. She looked back at her mother and signed something.

"What did she say?"

"She said it depends on your force of will. You can prolong your life if you truly desire to live longer. You can outrun time for a while, but it will catch you. If you give up on life, you could die in your sleep tonight."

He smiled at the little sprite, captivated. "I think I need to learn your language, Tesla. You could teach me some things."

She grinned and signed fast at her mother. Forest nodded.

"She asked me if it's all right if you stay with us for the night."

"Oh...I'm flattered." And he was, deeply. "But maybe you should ask your dad if it's okay with him."

Tesla turned on her heel and headed to the other room where Syrus was talking to Rahaxeris.

"He'll agree," Forest said. "He can't deny her anything. It's kind of pathetic how wrapped around her finger he is."

He smirked and nodded. "Those are cunning little fingers...I really wasn't expecting an invitation. It's awkward, right? I can come up with an excuse why I can't stay."

"It is a bit awkward, I'll admit."

"Okay. I'll tell her I can't."

She narrowed her eyes. "Where have you been staying?"

"Maxcarion's old place. It's plenty comfortable, and it keeps me close to the Lair. Close to..."

"Close to her," she finished for him. "A she-wolf, huh? What's her name? I bet I know her."

The heat rose in his cheeks, and he shook his head.

"Not saying?" She smirked. "Okay. Keep your secret."

He sighed, trying to force his heart to let go of Sabra. "It's foolish of me. It's over between us, whatever it was."

"Would you like to stay with us tonight?"

He tried to analyze how he felt. "Yeah. I would."

"Then stay. You won't be the first vagabond to sleep on my couch." Forest smiled.

"Dinner's ready." Syrus poked his head into the room.

Sitting at a dinner table with good people, eating and conversing easily, made Shreve feel as though he was walking through a dream. This couldn't be happening to him. It felt so good, foreign, and terrifying all at once. Part of him didn't believe he was actually awake. Maybe he was still under the hypnotic power of that Storyteller. He saw things, the invisible ties between the other adults at the table. Copernicus was a fool to think he was strong enough to sever these cords. They were impenetrable and immortal.

After dinner, Tesla began to yawn.

"It's time for bed," Syrus told her.

She signed something.

"No," Forest said.

She signed something else and, from her face and body language, Shreve got the impression she was whining.

"No," Syrus answered her this time.

She threw up her hands dramatically and rolled her eyes before climbing down from her chair. To his delight, she came over to him and held out her hands. Shreve took them, her power shoving its way into him again. When she pulled her hands free of his, she wrapped her arms around his neck. He was shocked and again his heart swelled. The little sprite was hugging him.

She bolted out of the room, her long, dark tresses flowing after her.

"Hey!" Rahaxeris called after her. "You didn't tell anyone else goodnight!"

Syrus got up from the table and followed Tesla. In a few minutes, they were back. Her eyes were drooping, and she yawned as she clung to a fuzzy yellow blanket.

"Well, go on," Syrus said to her.

She came back over to Shreve and thrust the blanket at him.

He took it, bemused. "Umm... What's this?"

"That's her favorite blanket. She insisted you have it tonight, since you're not at your home and might need something comforting."

Everyone's attention settled on him. "Thank you," he said, quickly.

She hugged him again before kissing Forest and Rahaxeris in turn, then taking her father's hand and heading back to her room.

The pressure in his temples was unbearable. "Excuse me, I just...need some air."

He got up, set the blanket on the chair, and strode quickly from the house, out into the garden. The cool night air caressed his face, and he exhaled. The breeze chilled the tears on his cheeks. He wiped them off with the back of his hand. He was growing a thick layer of understanding. Love, family, home, truth...

These were the things people fought and died for willingly. These were the things he never had and was taught to hate and destroy. It only took an open door, a meal, a little girl willing to sacrifice her comfort to give him some, and he was completely unmade.

He didn't realize how long he stood there, until the lights in the windows began to go out, and Rahaxeris came out into the garden.

"A lot to process?" Rahaxeris asked.

"You could say that."

"I know. It was for me, too, still is sometimes."

"What do you mean?"

Rahaxeris smiled. "Look at me. I was the high priest of the *Rune-dy*. My life didn't have any soft edges to it. I'd loved Forest since she was a baby, but I never imagined she would love me back. Never. Have you noticed she calls me Dad?"

"Yeah. I heard her."

"She didn't used to. It's kind of a new thing, but I hope she keeps it up."

Shreve shook his head and frowned. "So strange. I wouldn't have ever believed I had these places inside me. Weaknesses. I used to think I was such a badass."

Rahaxeris laughed. "You still are, but now you have a heart... Take Syrus for example. His heart belongs to his family, and it's a big heart. But having seen him in action, especially in the last year, he takes badass to a new level.

"Having a heart doesn't rob you of your strength, Shreve. It gives you a purpose. If you must fight, if you must kill, you know the reason."

"I think I'm only starting to understand the difference."

"You understand it," Rahaxeris insisted. "I saw you in there with Tesla. I watched you transform. Just think, not that long ago, you were a part of the plot that hurt her, almost killed her. And now, what would you do to someone who threatened her?"

An acute bloodthirst seized him at the very idea. "I'd protect her. No matter what it cost me."

He laughed again and gave him a hearty slap on the back. "See? You understand." They stood in silence for a moment. "Will you help me protect Tesla from the coming army?"

"What can I do?" Shreve asked.

"I don't know yet. But I have a feeling you'll be needed in building our defenses."

"I'm at your disposal."

He smirked. "Not running off anywhere?"

"No. If I'm not near Forest, I'll be close to the Lair."

He walked a few paces and opened a portal. "I didn't realize what it would mean to me to have both of my children together." His voice was loud over the rushing. "In whatever detached, unnatural way, you are my son, Shreve."

Then he stepped into the portal and was gone.

Shreve went back into the house. It was quiet, and most of the lights were off. A pillow and the fuzzy yellow blanket were spread out on the couch for him. Light and soft voices were coming through the cracked bedroom door. Then Forest came out in a light pink shirt and a matching pair of shorts. He smirked as he read the words under the simple picture on her chest.

"Hello Kitty?" he chuckled.

She glanced down at her shirt and huffed. "Shut up. I'm going to bed now. Syrus won't be asleep for quite a while yet, but he'll be in here with me. Hopefully, Tesla will sleep soundly, but she can get loud in the middle of the night—just fair warning. Is there anything you need?"

"I'm overwhelmed and humbled by the trust you're showing me. It makes me think you're a little crazy."

She smirked. "I am crazy. Don't forget that. And you don't worry me overmuch. If you get squirrelly, you'll be hacked to bits, electrocuted, and then turned into a reanimated automaton."

"A what?"

Forest's smirk broadened into an evil smile. "Me and Syrus are the least of your problems. If you threaten us, it's Tesla you'll have to worry about."

His eyebrows shot up, and he glanced at the closed door of the little girl's room. "So noted."

He looked back at Forest, and her evil smile relaxed into a genuine one. "Thank you for staying."

So many things he could have said. Words that felt odd because he'd never used them. Instead, he just nodded and looked down. She accepted his silence.

"Goodnight." Her voice was soft.

She turned and went back to her room, leaving the door cracked as the light went out. He lay down on the couch and stared up at the ceiling for a long time, yet again wondering if he was dreaming. In a few short hours he had gained the titles guest, brother, uncle, and son. Syrus had been tolerant but more reserved than the rest of them. It was still better than he deserved, and he hoped he might live long enough to earn the mage's friendship.

Right before he drifted off to sleep, he imagined he had a home, just like this one. One he shared with Sabra. How amazing would it be to share your life like that? To be known intimately, fully for who he really was and loved because of it, or even in spite of it? To have children? As he imagined all these things, the well of sorrow within him dug itself deeper.

CHAPTER THIRTEEN

After a week, Sabra finally decided to get on with her life and continue her training. Throughout those days and nights, she'd stayed locked in her room, Gahu had yet to come back. Or maybe he had, but she'd barely heard the occasional beating on her door. Tucker would yell at her a couple of times a day, but she ignored him.

A phantom of Shreve had taken up residence in her room. Sometimes he wore the face she loved, sometimes not. He didn't speak to her. At night, in that place between being awake and dreaming, the phantom touched her. She could almost feel his hands on her body, his lips on her skin. Guilt-ridden, she'd bat him away, or pull him closer and let him take her over like the hot flash of fever. The fact that she couldn't banish the apparition only brought her self-disgust.

She began to try to fight her constant thoughts of Shreve by refocusing her mind on tactical training for the tournament. It was a non-stop tug of war, and she had yet to clear her mind of him completely for even a moment.

Before the pre-dawn, she slunk from the apartment and ran through the shadows, away from the Lair, to the shifter colony. Nothing had changed there. Her weapons were hidden in the same place. Again, she felt guilty. Guilty that she had let Asher down by holing up in her room and moping for so long. She was done with that. She was done with thinking about Shreve. Really, she was. No, really.

She paced a few minutes, wrestling with her memory of when she'd caught Shreve here in the dark, and he'd given her the sword. Pissed he wouldn't get out of her head, she began warming up and sparring with his phantom. She threw punches, rolled, and spun through the air in aerial kicks.

Heart in her throat, breathing hard, she swung out at nothing. Asher came out of nowhere and caught her fist. She dropped her attack stance.

"Didn't know if you were ever going to come back," he said.

"I'm sorry. That won't happen again. I'm here. I'm ready."

"I can see that. I'm glad you haven't given up."

"My resolve has never been stronger. So, what are we going to work on today?"

Asher smiled sadly. "Are you all right?"

"Of course. Why wouldn't I be?"

"Shreve."

She winced and swore. She considered just lying, and covering with bravado. Instead, she hung her head and closed her eyes. "Have you seen him?"

"Two days ago. He's in a bad way. He's hurting."

"Well, good!"

Asher smirked. "Uh huh."

"What does that mean?" she demanded.

"Nothing." He was glib.

"Am I training today, or not?"

"Sure. Get your whip."

Asher backed out of the space, where her whip wouldn't hit him. He directed her from the sidelines. Now she didn't envision Shreve as her opponent, it was Gahu. Her anger rose up as she thought of the way he had treated her the last time. It was the first time she'd really thought about what it would be like to face him in the tournament. It was the first time she felt she *could* take him out.

The whip was more than an extension of her arm, it was an extension of her will. The leather unrolled through the air, the tip snapping the exact point she wanted to hit on the charred house, splintering the wood. Her focus was razor sharp. Adrenaline compressed her drive till it became clear and hardened like a diamond. She pushed her body, time blurring in the background. Over and over she raised her arm, and the whip struck out at objects. She was determined to break her target to nothing.

"Sabra!" Asher yelled, breaking into her focus. "You've lost track of time. You better get going, or you risk discovery."

She looked up at the sky. Where had the time gone? He was more than right. Reluctantly, she coiled her whip and put it away.

"Thank you, Asher." She began sprinting away.

"I forgot. There's something I need to talk to you about, but it's too late now. Remind me tomorrow first thing. It's important."

"Okay." She waved and kept going.

Damn, she was running late. No big deal, she thought. But there were a few people moving around the square as she ran through to the mountain's entrance. People considered her eccentric anyway, she tried to comfort herself. But as she came through the front door, sweaty and out of breath, her stomach dropped. Tucker was right there in the living room, and she knew from the look on his face, she was in trouble.

"Tucker, I—" Her voice turned into a wheeze as he plowed his fist into her stomach.

When she doubled over, he grabbed her by the hair, yanked her up again, and slapped her so hard in the face she went spinning to the floor. She gasped and spit the blood from her mouth.

"I can no longer tolerate your behavior. You are on the edge of ruining our family name forever."

"What did I do?!"

"Gossip about you is rampant. You never removed your name from the tournament list. And somehow, it's gotten around that you're playing the whore."

"Who says that? Silhon?"

The look in his eye confirmed it, even though he didn't answer the question. "It doesn't matter who says it, because now everyone believes it. I honestly can't believe Gahu hasn't backed out yet."

"I wish he would!" she spat.

"Really?" he scoffed. "Because if he does, I've been given another offer for you."

"I bet! By the one spreading the rumors!"

"That's right. Now lower your tone, or I'll choke it down!"

She looked up at him, seeing only red. "Just because our laws allow you to treat me this way doesn't make it right. You're not any better than me because you're male. You're not smarter, braver. You're certainly not kinder. I don't recognize your, or any other man's, authority over me."

"Bitch! Those words could get you killed."

She only had a split second to decide what she was going to do. If she fought, he'd lock her in the underground, and she'd never be able to fight in the tournament then. Cowering submission was more bitter than poison, but it was the only way she'd see herself through this day, with blackened eyes no doubt. He bore down on her, and she took it, even though she could have kicked his ass easily.

He was relentless and brutal. Her heart broke as she realized in that moment she had lost her brother. He was the last living member of her family, and now, he was dead to her as well. The pain of the realization mixed in with the pain he inflicted on her until he finally hit her hard enough to knock her unconscious.

Time moved, and she lost it as it went by. Sabra opened her eyes very slowly. Both were swollen. The dancing jeweled colors of the sunset moved over her. The whole day was gone. She moved slightly, feeling her limbs. The cold hard rock under her kissed her with soreness. The bastard had dragged her out onto the terrace and just left her there. Her heart smarted again. When had her brother traded his good nature for cruelty?

She rose into a sitting position, gritting her teeth as her head hammered. What her brother had done to her was typical behavior of wolf men. Accepted if not encouraged. Her cheeks burned even though she was alone. She wasn't designed for this degradation. No she-wolf was. It was coming to an end soon. Oh, yes. It was going to end!

She got to her feet and took a few testing steps. It wasn't that bad. A little food and water, a small rest in her actual bed, and she'd be just fine. Was that the best he could do to someone who wasn't fighting back? Coward. He wasn't a man. Male, yes. Man, no.

She made to go in and take care of herself but found the doors locked. Nasty move by Tucker. She stretched and took a few deep breaths before kicking the doors inward. They swung in, the frame splintering around the knobs. The doors banged loudly against the walls. She stalked inside and looked around. Tucker wasn't there.

Her throat was so dry, the first gulp of water she took seemed to shred and burn all the way down. The second gulp was soothing. She splashed water on her abused face and looked in the mirror. Dried blood clung to the edges of her mouth and circled the insides of her nostrils. As she suspected, both of her eyes were black, and one of her cheeks was swollen.

She ate cold leftovers and stale bread and locked herself in her room before Tucker came back. Her shirt was stained with blood, totally ruined. Too many of her clothes had to be discarded from blood stains, she lamented. Sabra stripped down to nothing and took stock of her body. She was all right, just sore. He hadn't broken any bones.

She slipped into a pair of soft drawstring pants and a loose-fitting shirt before lying down on her bed. What did she do now? How did she play her hand? What had gotten into Silhon? She guessed she underestimated his desire for her, aberrant as it was. Would Gahu believe the rumors?

She squirmed as she thought back to the last time she'd seen him. He knew her body was on fire, and she'd admitted it wasn't for him. Would he think she had a lover? Was Silhon claiming he was the one she'd been messing around with? Ugh...what did she do with all this?

There was still too much time until the tournament for her to just hide, play sick, or hold Gahu at arm's length. She'd have to give in to him physically, or... Could she run away? If she did, she could live for herself, but she would be abandoning the other women.

Sabra suddenly became exceedingly angry. Why was she the only one fighting against the abuse? Did none of the other she-wolves have a spine at all? How could she be expected to carry the whole load of this? Why did she have to forfeit her life, when no one else was willing to risk anything?

She contemplated the feeling of her heart, thumping against her ribs. That was all she had left. Just her life. She had no family anymore. Tucker was dead to her. She despised Gahu. She pinched her eyes shut and saw Shreve in his wolf form. He'd never treat her like a possession, with no soul, designed only for pleasure and breeding, to be beaten and caged when she displeased him. Or publicly humiliated for the fun of it.

Her body remembered how it felt to run with him. Just the two of them, under the moon, totally free for a short time. Connected, honest, primal. She wanted to feel that again. She wanted the honesty of it. Her hate for him was honest as well. He knew it. Her heart flinched, and chills surfaced on her skin as the memory of his voice calling for her reverberated through her mind.

She never wanted to see him again as a man...but as a wolf. That was the truth she craved but would never indulge in. She would make her heart an island, solitary and impossible to reach.

She was juggling a pack of lies, detesting each one more than the last. It was time to let them fall and break. They had pushed her too far. She would live true to herself, or not at all.

She looked through her window, at the sky. One hour till the moon would be visible over the top of the forest. She'd sleep one hour, to heal. Then she'd begin living as she chose. Perhaps that decision would mean she'd die before the sunrise. So be it.

Sabra overslept by a few minutes only and woke completely healed from Tucker's punishment. Adrenaline spiked as she got out of bed. She hadn't realized the weight she'd been carrying around, until now. Letting it all go, she could have floated off the floor.

What was she going to do, exactly? She realized she didn't know as she got a knapsack and began putting a few clothes into it. She had Knick-knacks, a few pieces of jewelry, but... Wherever she was going, all she needed were the bare essentials. She could leave it all behind.

Where was she going? She thought about Paradigm. All races were welcome there. But what if she left without really leaving? She could wait out the time until the tournament. Her name was still on the list, because no one could take it off, but her.

She stiffened as she heard Tucker come home. Maybe he would leave her alone, but if he didn't... She strapped on her boots and latched a dagger belt around her waist. She tied a tight knot in the top of her knapsack and took it to the window. She looked down. The square was empty. She held her breath and let it drop, praying it wouldn't be discovered, or taken, before she could get to it.

Tucker pounded on her door. Her heart hardened. This was it. She called on all of her courage, took a deep breath, and opened the door. He looked surprised for a second, as though he hadn't expected her to open the door.

"Um...come out here. We need to talk."

She managed to smile. "We certainly do."

She walked past him and sat down on the couch. He gazed at her suspiciously as he sat down opposite her.

"Gahu will be here in a few minutes. Things are going to change tonight, and you better go along with them, and act happy, or it will be the worst for you."

"What changes?" Her tone was mild, almost bored.

"You don't live here anymore. Gahu is coming to collect you. You will move in with him tonight. It might be slightly frowned on before your mating ceremony, but only slightly. I doubt anyone will say anything."

"Really? You doubt it?"

"Yeah, since you have no more reputation, except a tainted one. This will end that, and in everyone's mind, put you securely as Gahu's woman… He's lost enough face over your behavior." He leaned forward and pointed his finger at her. "If you fight this, or even complain once, he said he's going to abandon you. If that happens, I'll disown you, and Silhon will use you for his amusement, no doubt. Once he's done with you, you'll be passed around and used like trash. Just think about that when you go with Gahu. Your future depends on you making him happy tonight. You better give him everything, and I mean everything, he wants and more."

"How long before he gets here?"

"Any moment now."

"Okay," she said mildly as she stood. "I guess I better gather my things, so I don't keep him waiting."

She walked back into her room, but instead of gathering anything, she grabbed a scrap of paper and scrawled a quick note to Gahu. She rolled the paper and put it inside the wooden cuff he'd given her and set it on the center of her bed.

She strode back out into the living room. Tucker hadn't moved. She grabbed his hand and pulled him to his feet.

"What?" he said.

She hugged him. He hesitated for a second before patting her back awkwardly. She let go and took a step back.

"I hope one day you will find your goodness again."

"Wha—" He choked on the word as her fist slammed into his throat.

Before he could draw breath, she head-butted him. His head snapped back, and he staggered. He roared and fought to focus his spinning eyes on her. She kicked him in the knee, jumped behind as he fell sideways, and wrapped her arm around his neck. She pulled with all her might. He struggled for only a few seconds, pulling at her forearm, his heel scraping the floor. And then he went limp. She lowered him to the floor.

"Goodbye, Tucker. When you wake up, you'll know just how submissive I've been. I could have bested you any time."

A knock came on the front door. Damn. Out of time. She ran to the broken terrace doors and out. The knocking grew impatient as she jumped over the rails. Pain spiked in her ankles as she hit the ground and took off running. She went straight through the square, grabbing the knapsack and slinging it across her back without losing stride.

When she broke the boundary of the Lair's suburbs, into the wilds, she ran faster for the pure maniacal joy of running free. No matter how long it lasted. She'd never felt like this. So light, as if she were a bird. It was just her, the wind, and the moon. Sabra couldn't remember having so much energy. It took no effort to run flat out all the way to the shifter colony.

She ducked into the skeleton of the house where her weapons were and sat down, leaning against the foundation blocks. Laughter poured from her lungs. What was she going to do now? She needed a new plan. Should she go to Paradigm? Or could she just stay right here? If she stayed in the shifter colony, this close to the Lair, would she be able to go undetected? Would anyone take the trouble to look for her? She really had no idea.

She wanted to stay close, so she could still know what was going on and be ready to step in when the tournament began. Her heart wasn't willing to let go of her dream of leading the pack. She just needed to stay out of sight until then.

Her excitement began to ebb. The night was still young. Asher wouldn't arrive until right before sunrise. She needed his help, now more than ever. She knew he would be willing, but would he be successful? If anyone decided to look for her, he could lead them away with lies, false evidence, and misdirection. Then she could stay right there, under their noses, and bide her time.

The moon shone on her through the open roof, and its pull reached down deep inside her. The animal within shivered. *What are you waiting for? Are you going to live free or not?* She stood, took her clothes off, and put them in her sack. She ran her fingers through the length of her hair.

Don't tempt me so brazenly. That's what Shreve had said.

Brazen, yes that's what she was. A smile curved her lips. Then she called to the wolf inside and let it out. A shiver rolled through her whole body down to her bones as she shifted. It felt so good to be free like this, she thought as she ran. But the careless, free feeling didn't last long, and soon she began to search for him. She didn't mean to, but her ears pricked at every miniscule sound, and her nostrils flared, sniffing intently at the air.

She wanted to run with him again—she couldn't deny it. She continued to seek him as she made her way to the place where she'd first seen him. Nothing. She went to the river. Again nothing. No trace at all. Compelled and hating she was compelled, she shifted back into a woman when she came to the place they had kissed.

The night air caressed her naked skin and combed through her hair. She paced among the thick trees, touching the bark lightly with her hands. What did she want from him? Nothing! She blew out a breath and shook her head. She couldn't even convince herself of that. If she truly wanted nothing, why was she here?

"Who are you, Shreve?" she whispered. "Why did you try to help me?"

It was the first time she'd really dissected her encounters with him. He'd been a member of the Aluka Circle. So had others. They had been forced. Made into slaves. Had he? She latched onto that thought. If he had been forced, then he wasn't responsible for Sophie in any way. He felt guilty. He was sorry. He'd said so, but she'd also felt it when they were connected as wolves and there was no way to lie. Had she been unfair to him?

He had helped her, she thought again. The whip, the sword. He was an outsider. She didn't even understand his racial background. He was a wolf, but he could shift, too. Her thoughts circled. She sighed and pushed her hair back from her face. She'd run with him, for goodness sake! She knew him on that elemental level.

Asher liked him. That carried weight with her.

She shivered and rubbed her arms. Her heart groaned in frustration and indecision. Sophie came to her mind. What would Sophie tell her to do if she were here now?

She knew. She shifted back into a wolf, ready to run again. Ready to feel her freedom and commune with the moon.

When, if, she saw him again, she'd let him talk. She'd ask him what she needed to know, and she'd listen. After that, she didn't know.

CHAPTER FOURTEEN

Zeren, Syrus, Redge, Journey, Merhl, and Shreve came into the main chamber of *Rune-dy* headquarters as Rahaxeris had requested. Syrus had forewarned Zeren and Merhl about Shreve's presence. They had accepted it, *very* reluctantly, and were obviously on edge around him.

Rahaxeris laid the cube on the table for the group to see and explained what he knew about it. No one approached it, except Merhl, who braced his gnarled hands on the table and leaned down toward it. He pursed his lips as he turned it around with just the tip of his index finger.

"It's made of the same material as Netriet's arm."

"Yes. It's from the same world," Rahaxeris confirmed.

Journey moved forward, a hesitant but excited light in her eyes. "Merhl?"

He looked at her.

"Remember what we talked about?"

He nodded slowly, and then his eyes widened, and he looked back at the cube.

Before anyone could gripe that they needed to be filled in on their little secret, Journey spoke.

"I've been talking with the Heart. I've made some real progress healing it. We have a relationship. I wouldn't go so far as to call it friendship, but almost. If this tesseract truly is a power harness, nothing in Regia has more power than the Heart. We must put the cube in the flames. I'll talk to it. Persuade the Heart to accept it."

"No," Merhl said. "You can talk to the Heart, but it's not going to be as simple as just throwing the cube into the flames. We can't put the cube anywhere near the Heart until I've opened it and…"

"What?" Rahaxeris demanded.

Merhl sighed. "After all this time. Since we found out the wizards were coming. I've been pushing myself to create something new, and I have, but I keep going back to the same thing. A blood lock."

"But you made a blood lock around Forest," Syrus said. "And it didn't work. Copernicus was able to break it."

"Yes," Merhl admitted. "This would be a reverse blood lock, not one to hold in, but to keep out. If I were to try to make the same kind as the one I put around Forest, I'd have to put the blood of every Regian inside it. And the wizards would break through anyway…" He picked up the cube. "I will make the blood lock inside this. And I only need blood from one wizard. The lock will hold them back. Wizard blood will not be able to cross it. See?"

Everyone nodded.

"I wouldn't trust it to last long," he continued. "But once it's constructed, if we have the Heart powering the lock…" He broke off and sighed. "I've got nothing else. I'm sorry. I feel this will work, or buy us some more time at least."

Journey put her hand on his shoulder. "You've done well, Merhl."

"Yeah, um…" Redge came forward from where he was leaning against the wall. "I hate to be the bearer of bad news, but there are no more wizards in Regia."

Shreve swallowed. "There's me. But my blood is mixed."

"That won't do. For the lock to work, the blood must be wizard only," Merhl said.

The group launched into a passionate discussion about whether they were certain there were no more wizards in Regia. Rahaxeris took Shreve's arm and led him into another room and closed the door.

"Redge is correct. There are no more wizards." Rahaxeris' voice was sorrowful. "I can extract your wizard DNA and separate it from your other blood types, but…"

Shreve took a deep breath. "But the extraction will kill me?"

"I don't know the odds, but they are long. I can't give you any hope that you would survive the operation."

"The blood lock is a good plan. The only one there is, it seems."

"This is your choice, Shreve."

Shreve closed his eyes. He was almost out of time anyway. If he did this, if it worked, he'd achieve what he wanted. The only thing he desired more than Sabra. If he could save Regia, surely that would be enough to redeem him from his crimes. He could be forgiven.

His idea of saving everyone shrank down into a smaller and smaller point, until all he saw was Sabra. He'd give anything to save her. He opened his eyes. "I'll do it…I just… Can I say goodbye to someone first?"

The depth of sorrow he saw in Rahaxeris pulled at his heart. "Let's talk to Merhl about buying you as much time as you need. I don't want you robbed of even one day."

They went back out to the still arguing group. Rahaxeris began explaining things to them. Shreve couldn't hear it. His ears filled with white noise, and he looked down. He could feel their eyes on him. He could feel the shift in their gazes as Rahaxeris spoke. They were all looking at him with emotions that had never been applied to him. He forced himself to look up. Yes, there it was in their eyes. Admiration, respect, and gratitude. He was their champion.

His ears cleared as Merhl spoke to him.

"As soon as I leave here, I will set up a series of alarms. I will make sure I place them so far out that if the wizards begin their approach, we will have two days, maybe more, to finish the blood lock before they get here."

Rahaxeris placed his long, sharp hand on Shreve's shoulder. "Go. Close the last chapter of your life in the way you choose. When the time comes, I will send for you."

"Please open a portal for me to the wilds near the Lair."

Rahaxeris took a step back and struck the air, opening a portal for Shreve.

The group remained for a while, but Rahaxeris was anxious for them all to leave, except Merhl. He wasn't going to let the cube leave *Rune-dy* headquarters, and so Merhl was going to be a permanent fixture while he worked on it. As the group dispersed, Rahaxeris held Syrus back.

"Please bring Tesla here tomorrow. I need a few hours with her."

"Excellent! That means I get alone time with Forest. Gosh, it's been so long..."

Rahaxeris closed his eyes and shook his head at Syrus' exuberance. "Don't say anything else, Syrus. You're about to make it weird."

****

Sabra remained in wolf form most of the night. She ran herself out, as she experienced her emotions without thought or filter. The entire night was solitary. She encountered no one. When the moon began to set, she made her way back to the shifter colony.

She looked at it with new eyes. There was plenty of debris to salvage and move so she could actually make a shelter for herself. She shifted back into a woman and dressed quickly. She stiffened as she heard approaching footsteps and reached for her whip.

"Sabra?" Asher's voice was quiet, almost a whisper.

She relaxed and came out.

He looked relieved when he saw her. "I was afraid for you."

"Why?"

"*Why?*" he scoffed. "You ran away. If you were the talk of the Lair before, it's nothing to now. I was awakened from a dead sleep last night by Gahu, beating my door down, looking for you."

"Shit! I hoped he wouldn't care that much."

Asher scowled. "He was in a rage. It wasn't much of a lover's concern. He told me about what you did to Tucker. I feared maybe Silhon had done something."

"What did you fear I'd done, old man?" Silhon demanded loudly, stepping out from the thick of trees nearby. His gang followed, filtering through the forest.

Sabra froze inside, her hand tightened on the whip handle. They advanced, forming a closing semi-circle. She raised her arm and struck out. The whip crack was louder than any she'd done before. Each of the thugs halted and looked surprised. Silhon signaled for them to stop their approach.

Sabra ducked back into the house as fast as she could, grabbing her sword, and the broadsword, tossing it to Asher. They stood together, back to back.

"Back off!" she ordered, rolling her wrist side to side, making the whip dance along the ground. "Or I'll snap your pretty eyes out first, Silhon."

He smirked. "Give it up. You've got no chance... Of course, what am I thinking? You'd never give up, would you? I would hate for you to anyway. You'll fight, just as I want you to." He cupped himself lewdly. "So much sweeter that way. I know you will be, once I've put you in your place, underneath me."

"The only way you'll get me under you is if I'm dead."

"Come now. I know this is what you wanted all along. You're wasted with Gahu. He'd have no idea what to do with you. Not like I do. You knew it would come to this."

His smile grew bigger, and he drew his sword, nodding at the others to do the same. She cracked her whip again in warning. It bought them only a second.

"Run, Sabra," Asher whispered.

"Never!"

It was seven against two. She didn't waste time thinking it was hopeless. She set her sights on Silhon.

"Come on, bitch!" she yelled.

The whole gang gasped and looked at him. She'd called him the worst, most insulting, taboo thing a woman could say to a man in wolf culture.

He blinked three times, looking winded, before his smile came back. "Stop begging me for it, Sabra."

The gang rushed them. Instant chaos as the sounds of clanging metal filled the air. Asher took two out at once with one long sweep of his sword. The blade cutting across first one throat and then the other in turn. Sabra struck out with her whip, catching Silhon on the shoulder. The hook on the end caught his flesh and tore a nasty hole as she yanked the leather back to her.

He yelled out in pain and hung back from the group, holding his hand over the bleeding gash. The rest were too close for the whip now. She dropped it and parried a sloppy strike with her katana. She felt Asher's back press against hers. Only three of them were fighting now. Silhon wasn't the only one keeping his distance. His henchman, Gareth, also wasn't engaging.

She caught her opponent with an upswing, knocking his sword from his hands. Her blade slid into his chest. It was the first time she'd killed anyone, but she didn't have time to contemplate it. Before she could push his body off her sword, the bastard behind him struck out at her. She ducked, but caught his sword with her forearm. The blade cut through her muscles and tendons down to the bone. She heard the sound of a knife as it flew through the air, but she never saw it. All she knew was she was now alone, fighting.

They'd gotten Asher. Rage and agony blinded her. She couldn't feel the pain as she cut the one in front of her from collarbone to groin. Just three left.

The one she fought now was more skilled than the others, and

Gareth was coming forward now, while Silhon still hesitated.

"Don't kill her!" Silhon shouted. "She's mine."

A blast threw her backward, her sword flew from her hand as she hit the ground. She looked up. Shreve came out of nowhere. The one she'd been fighting struck at him. He grabbed his arm and took his sword from his hand as if he had no more strength than a baby. Shreve cut his head off quickly.

She scrambled to get up and get her sword. When she turned back around, Silhon slammed into her, knocking her back on the ground and pinning her under him. "You've done better than I thought you would. Let's finish this."

He hauled her up, spun her around so she was facing away from him, and held a knife to her throat.

Shreve and Gareth were circling each other.

"Hey!" Silhon yelled.

****

Shreve looked over at Sabra and her captor for a split second, gaging the danger of the situation, and turned his attention back to Gareth. She could handle the bastard holding her without his help. Gareth had to be neutralized in the shortest order. He didn't have time to screw around with him.

Gareth moved first, and damn if he wasn't fast. Shreve focused on pulling from his ogre blood, knowing the split second distraction would cost him. Shreve's hand transformed as Gareth's sword plunged into his stomach and up. The blade slid up through him until the tip pierced his heart. Shreve put his hand flat on Gareth's chest and opened a portal. His heart and lungs were sucked straight out of him, leaving a huge empty hole in his torso. Gareth and Shreve fell to the ground together.

"*NO!*" Sabra's scream filled his ears.

He heard her scuffle with Silhon and opened his eyes in time to see him fall. The blade he'd held to her throat now hilt-deep in his eye. Then she was leaning over Shreve, pulling Gareth's sword out. Damn, that burned.

She grabbed at his wound and tried to hold it together. "No, please, please, please, no."

He put his hands over hers to still them. Her eyes were unfathomable as she looked down at him. She didn't want him to die. That knowledge alone gave him the strength to use the power of his wizard blood to heal himself.

Her mouth fell open as the wound sealed up, not even leaving a scar. His heart labored under the use of magic. Knowing he'd just knocked more hours, or days even, off of his life, he sat up.

"Are you hurt?" he asked.

"Am I hurt?"

Shreve looked over the bodies, his eyes landing on Asher. "No." His voice came out weak. He scrambled up and ran over to Asher, falling on his knees next to him. He shook him and felt for a pulse. He was dead. Shreve pulled the knife out of his chest, his vision blurring with tears.

Shreve hung his head and wept. Sabra came up behind him and put her hands on his shaking shoulders for a moment, then she was on her knees next to him, crying also. For a while they just stayed like that, grieving in silence, side by side.

She reached over and closed Asher's eyes. "I swore I'd never cry again. I swore to Sophie, the day after she died. This is the second time I've broken that oath...I also swore I'd never see you again."

Shreve swallowed and nodded. "I'll leave as quickly as I can."

She grabbed his hand and shook her head. "That's not what I meant."

He pulled her hand up, looking at the wound on her arm. "Hold your arm straight."

She obeyed. He pulled his blood-stained, ripped shirt over his head and tore the fabric into a strip. He wrapped it tight around her arm and tied a knot. "How long will it take you to heal from that?"

"It's really deep. A full day, maybe longer. Not sure."

It hurt so much for him to be so close to her. He stood and walked away from the mess of bodies. "What is this going to mean for you? All this death?"

She followed him. "I don't know... This wouldn't have happened, or *probably* wouldn't have happened if I hadn't run away last night."

He faced her. "What do you mean?"

She scrubbed a hand over her face and blew out a breath. "I decided to leave the Lair. Live life on my own terms. My brother was kicking me out of our home, trying to force me to move in with Gahu...I...I just had enough of being pushed around and beaten...I thought maybe I could lay low until the tournament, but I didn't realize..." She looked back at the carnage and shivered as though cold.

Shreve didn't know what to say. He just stared at her desperately, wishing he could hold her.

She laughed darkly. "I never knew how desirable I was. I had no idea Silhon wanted me that badly." Then she was crying again. "And now Asher's dead, and it's my fault."

He took a step toward her, and then stopped. She looked at him, wiped the tears on her cheeks, and stepped into his space. She laid her head against his shoulder and wrapped her arms around his waist. He held her back, resting his cheek on the top of her head. Comfort and grief mixed together and flowed from her into him and then back again.

He looked up at the Lair. "Don't go back there, Sabra. They'll blame you for this, call you a murderer."

"I know. You saved my life for no reason. They are going to kill me anyway."

His hands tightened on her arms. "Come with me."

She pulled away from him, shaking her head. "I have to honor Asher."

"Honor him with your life, not your death. Honor him by staying alive and fulfilling your destiny as pack leader. It's what he was striving to help you achieve. Honor him with winning the tournament."

She looked back at where Asher lay, her eyes tunneling.

"Please, Sabra..."Emotion threatened to crush him. "Don't choose death. Come with me."

The whole world came crashing down around him as she walked away.

She moved through the dead, picked up her sword and whip from the ground, and ducked into one of the houses. She came back out a second later, a pack on her back. Across the distance, their eyes met. She looked lost. For a minute she stood still, just staring at him. Then she slowly walked directly back to him.

"Okay. Where are we going?"

"Let's just get out of the open for a while and figure out what's the best move. The place I've been staying in the Wood is well hidden and not far away."

"Okay," she said again, flatly. Her eyes still looked tunneled.

He wanted to take her hand but resisted the urge. The only reason she was going with him was she had no other alternative at the moment, he reminded himself. So he walked on, and she followed a step behind. He glanced at her often.

The whole situation was terrible. For so many reasons, he wished what just happened, hadn't. She was injured, probably in shock, and they both had just lost their friend. He'd come to tell her goodbye, and he would, but it was going to take longer than he thought. He would see her through this and make sure she was safe. He hated the hollow look in her eyes.

When they crossed into the Wood, she roused a little from her blankness and looked around. He didn't give any thought to keeping on a trail. He didn't think about protecting her from the shadow sand until it was too late.

She stopped walking and leaned against a tree.

"Sabra?"

She sort of looked at him; her eyes were dilated and practically spinning. "It's your fault," she pointed at him drunkenly.

"What is?"

"I couldn't have sex with Gahu. And he's pretty hot. Not hot like you. No one's as hot as you. Ugh…" She shivered. "You ruined me. His touch felt nasty after yours. I wanted you, not him." She giggled. "You called me brazen. I like that. It's true… Typical wolf men…Silhon…my brother beat me…I have to help the women…"

He couldn't follow what she was saying. "Sabra, we have to keep going. We're almost there. You're just tripping on the sand."

She plunked down on her butt. "Why are you here?"

"I came to say goodbye."

She shook her head and giggled again. "Nope. Lies all lies!" She pointed at his chest. "You're in love with me."

He sighed, came forward, and picked her up. He'd have to carry her the rest of the way. She clung around his neck. Her head slumped on his shoulder. She began running her fingers lightly along his collarbone.

"I like your skin, Shreve… Why did you take your shirt off?"

"To make a bandage for you."

"Oh…I got it wrong."

He tried to ignore her touch as he carried her. Tried and failed.

"Got what wrong?" he knew he shouldn't ask.

"In my fantasies of you. I got your chest wrong. It's much nicer in real life."

"Fantasies?"

"Oh, yeah..." She drew the words out slowly and seductively. "The things you do to me...then I feel guilty, 'cause of Sophie." Her fingers began moving in little circles.

His breathing grew ragged. When she pressed her lips against his neck, he swore. "Stop that."

She laughed. "Bossy male. Typical."

"I am not typical."

"Oh, really?"

He had nowhere to shelter from her, except behind anger. "Yeah, really. If I was typical, I'd take you right now. You're intoxicated and asking for it. And yes, I really want to give it to you. It would be so easy. But then what? You wouldn't remember it, or if you did, you'd hate me for it."

Her silliness vanished, and she began crying, making him swear again.

"I hate you! It doesn't matter what you do, I hate you so much! Know why?"

"I know why." His voice was quiet.

"Oh? You know I hate you because you made me love you? You know that?"

He stopped walking and stared at her. "Sabra..."

She lifted her head off his shoulder and tried to look him in the eye. She blinked a few times, slowly. She put her head back down and closed her eyes. "Where are we?" Her voice went sleepy. "My arm hurts. Did you kidnap me?"

He blew out a breath and kept walking. "I stole you."

"Yes," she whispered. "Thief...beautiful...beautiful thief."

He couldn't help but feel relief when she fell asleep. She was killing him with her inebriated talking. He took her through the hidden doorway and laid her down face-up on the mat on the floor. He gently straightened her injured arm out. He placed her pack and weapons across the room and walked back outside.

Everything she'd said since they'd entered the Wood was now chiseled permanently in his brain. He'd thought she put his body on edge before, but he realized that was nothing compared to what she'd just done. He looked up at the morning sky and took a few deep breaths, striving for his system to ease back.

Shreve paced, the morning breeze chilling his bare chest. Dried blood covered his hands. He looked in the direction of the river and began walking toward it. When he reached the bank, he dove in. The water was cold, shocked all the heat from his body, and washed the blood away. He stroked to the surface, her voice in his head.

You know I hate you because you made me love you? You know that?

He pulled himself up on a boulder and sat, his feet hanging in the water. Did she love him? Was that the truth? But she'd said she hated him. He knew *that* was the truth. Was it possible to hate someone and love them at the same time? That made no sense to him. Maybe it was a capacity only women had.

I hate you because you made me love you.

Shreve couldn't help grinning like a fool. She wouldn't remember saying it, and that was probably for the best. But the words were his now, and he'd hold on to them for the rest of his life.

Behind the boulder, a shallow place pooled away from the current. He glanced down and saw his reflection. His mouth parted as he gaped at it. This must be the face Sabra saw. He touched his cheek as he recognized parts of this face. The eyes—they matched Forest's. The cheekbones were sharp like Rahaxeris'. His hair was black and wavy at the ends just above his shoulders, and there was a cleft in his chin. Was this his face? Had he found it? It held a family resemblance.

"I think I may have found myself," he said quietly to his reflection. "I think I might know who I am."

He jumped down and began walking back to his hiding place, water sloshing in his boots. Sabra was still out and would probably stay that way for a while yet. He changed into dry clothes and sat down in the chair, thinking about the fight they'd just been in. It wouldn't be long before the bodies were found. He had an idea.

He rummaged around until he found a scrap of paper and a pen.

Sabra,

Don't be alarmed if you wake up and don't remember how you got here, or even where you are. You got high on the sand, coming into the Wood. You're safe. Please don't leave. I've gone back to the Lair to learn what the reaction is when the bodies are discovered. We need information. I'll be back before dark. Please, please don't leave.

-Shreve

He laid the note on her chest and backed away, staring openly at her.

"You were right," he whispered. "I am in love with you. Very soon, I'm going to have to tell you that where you can hear me."

He pulled his elf blood forward and became invisible as he began walking back to the Lair. No one had discovered the bodies yet. He walked into the midst of the dead and examined the evidence of the scene. He carefully kept his eyes away from Asher's body.

He needed to confuse the scene and make sure there was no trace that would lead someone to Sabra. He moved a few of the bodies, so that it looked like they had turned on each other. He broke a branch off a tree and swept his and Sabra's footprints away. He carefully positioned himself and made a new set of footprints heading off in the other direction. He walked around in a large circle and then headed straight into the suburbs of the Lair.

Shreve slowed his pace, so as to not bump into anyone, and went to the public square. Sabra was all the talk with the men and women. The women had many ideas about what had happened to her.

"Do you really believe she ran away?"

"Do you think they killed her?" one whispered. "Her brother, or Gahu...or maybe it was Silhon, he saw her as a threat."

"I hope she's okay. Has anyone checked the underground?"

"I was there this morning—my sister's mate locked her up down there again. I was checking on her. I didn't see Sabra in any of the other cells."

"You don't think she'd abandon us, do you? We need her."

The oldest woman in the group spoke up. "If she is found or not, she was right. Things have to change. We have to make them change, no matter who our next leader is. Find your courage, girls. It's going to take all of us. We have to stand together and let the men know enough is enough."

Shreve moved away from them and was making his way over to a group of men, when Sabra's brother emerged from the mountain and climbed up on a huge boulder. Shreve knew it was her brother because he looked just like her. Another man came and stood next to the boulder, looking out on the crowd. He didn't know why, but something about the guy bothered him. Shreve hated him on sight.

"Listen to me!" her brother shouted. "You have all heard the rumors that my sister ran away last night. Gahu and I are forming a search party for her. We welcome any men who want to join us."

Ah ha. Shreve thought. No wonder I hate him, that's Gahu.

Four men came forward, but as they did, a boy ran into the square shouting at the top of his lungs. "Silhon is dead!" He pointed in the direction of the shifter colony. "There are bodies all over out there!"

Everyone began rushing toward the shifter colony.

"*STOP!*" A voice roared over the heads of the crowd.

They all stopped and turned back around. An old wolf was up on the boulder now.

"Everyone will stay here! I will investigate this."

173

The old man jumped down lithely and strode quickly out of the square. Murmurs erupted as soon as he was gone. Shreve moved over toward Gahu and Sabra's brother.

"What do you think?" Gahu asked quietly.

"I don't know. I can't imagine she could take out his entire gang. But perhaps Silhon is really dead. He wanted her, badly. She hated him... The way she attacked me last night... She could have killed me. I didn't know she had so much strength, or skill."

"I don't want you getting in my way when we find her," Gahu said. "I'm going to lock her in the underground and keep her there until I break her. It's too personal now. I'd walk away from her, but the damage she's done to my reputation...I can't let that pass."

"I understand," her brother said. "I won't stand in your way. She's yours to do with what you will."

Shreve moved away so he didn't give in to temptation and kill them both right there. He couldn't think of a reason why he shouldn't, so he retreated. He wanted to go back to Sabra, but he needed to wait to see what happened when the old wolf came back.

CHAPTER FIFTEEN

The ground reached up and began to pull Sabra under. Shreve had saved her life and paid with his own. *No, no, please, please! Don't die!* She pulled the sword out of him, his blood spilling over her hands. She grabbed at his wound, but it wouldn't close. Her tears blinded her. She couldn't see anything clearly. His heartbeat sounded in her ears, slowing, growing quiet as he bled out.

The anticipation held her immobile. There was nothing for her to do but wait. Now? One more beat? One more? The pain rose up like a demon in front of her. She waited, on the edge, with no choice. Shreve's heart stopped. She looked the pain straight on and braced herself as it slammed into her.

It threw her on her back. The first wave was like flash paper. A flame that rushed through her veins, burning every inch of her. Seared, then the heaviness began. Her heart strained against its natural function, questioning why. What was the point? Why continue when it hurt this much?

This was just the beginning of losing him. This was only the first moment. The first kiss of agony. The pain brought the unquestionable knowledge of how she truly felt. Only love, taken away, could leave this kind of pain behind. She couldn't deny it anymore. The pain stripped away the lies she'd told herself and forced her to know, to taste love and the living-death desolation of having it taken away.

"Shreve!" She woke up with a start, her eyes burning with tears.

She didn't know where she was. Her head hammered, and her arm burned. She took a few steadying breaths as she remembered the battle. She shook herself. Shreve wasn't dead, but Asher was. She pulled her knees up into her chest and looked around her. She spotted the note and lifted it up.

Sabra,

Don't be alarmed if you wake up and don't remember how you got here, or even where you are. You got high on the sand, coming into the Wood. You're safe. Please don't leave. I've gone back to the Lair to learn what the reaction is when the bodies are discovered. We need information. I'll be back before dark. Please, please don't leave.

-Shreve

She put the note down. High on sand? That was why she didn't remember how she'd gotten here. She pulled the bandage off and looked at her wound. It had pulled together, but it wouldn't be healed all the way for a few more hours. She stood up and looked around the space. It was oddly sparse. A few books and bottles inhabited a shelf. There was an armchair with ripped upholstery, and a few articles of clothing folded in a pile on the floor. She spotted her knapsack and weapons against the wall and felt a little steadier knowing she still had them.

How long had she been out? She didn't want to think about her dream, but it had changed things. The dream had taken off her blinders and revealed the truth. How was she going to handle being around him? When Gareth had stabbed him, when he'd fallen, when she'd held his wound with her hands, she got a taste of what she would feel if he died.

Her grievances against him faded into the background. She didn't have to sit around and contemplate forgiveness. She'd already given it. He wasn't the villain she'd thought he was. Not the villain perhaps that he'd been at one time. Her pride took a hit as she forced herself to really look at it. To really think about everything he'd ever said to her, everything he'd done. It wasn't a betrayal to love him. It was a betrayal to deny it. Sophie would have understood.

Since she had left her life at the Lair behind and Asher was dead, Shreve was all she had in the world. She couldn't bear to lose him now. But how did she move ahead? Was there any chance they could have a future? Would he still want her? There were things she needed to know. He had to tell her about his past and explain *what* he was.

She closed her eyes, goosebumps rising on her skin. When he came back, he had to kiss her. He had to touch her. She needed him to be her first. It had to be him. She couldn't give herself to anyone else. She sighed. She'd still make him work for it. He'd tell her everything first. Everything she needed and wanted to hear.

She needed some fresh air. She stepped outside and turned around, looking at the half-broken illusion hiding the door. The day was wearing thin. It was late afternoon. The sky would soon begin to dance with the colorful ribbons of dusk. She looked at the ground, trying to ascertain whether she was standing in shadow sand or not.

It looked okay. She'd have to pay attention. The wolves had come to the Wood all the time when Phillipe was the leader, but they all knew to keep to the paths to avoid the sand. Since he'd died, no one hardly went to the Wood at all anymore. At the moment, she was grateful the place was deserted.

Her attention snapped up at the sound of someone approaching. She held still, her eyes scanning, but she didn't see anyone. The noise kept getting closer and closer. Her heart beat hard and fast against her ribs.

Shreve materialized out of thin air forty feet in front of her. Their eyes held. It was all there. Everything she wanted to know. *He's all mine. To hell with making him work for it.* She ran at him. His eyebrows went up, and he braced himself as though he thought she was about to attack him. She jumped, threading herself around him. He staggered back a step, grabbing her hips.

She kissed him violently hard. "I love you."

He looked closely at her eyes. "Are you high again?"

"No."

She pressed tight against him, forcing her lips against his so he couldn't speak. He began to press back, a moan in the back of his throat. He let go of her hips, pushing her legs so she had to stand on the ground again. He reached around the back of his neck and pulled her hands loose, bringing them around to his face, breaking their kiss.

He kissed both of her hands. "Sabra, are you sure you're not high?"

"Look in my eyes."

He did. Her pupils were normal. He took a ragged breath. "I want…"

"What? Tell me what you want."

"You're so brazen."

Her voice turned into a dark whisper. "That's right. Tell me what you want."

"You said I had a nerve putting my hands on you."

She threaded her fingers through his and pulled his arms around her. "You do. A damn nerve. And since you're all tongue tied, I'll tell you what *I* want…I want a man who never loses his nerve."

He smiled and slid his hands down from her lower back, down to behind her knees, and picked her back up. She wrapped her legs around him the way they had been before. He took her through the hidden doorway and laid her down on the mat on the floor and covered her with his body.

A look of hesitation came over him then. "I didn't say it, not where you could hear me."

"What?"

"I'm in love with you, Sabra."

She smiled as she put her hands on his shoulders. "I know."

He closed his eyes. "I don't know if I can satisfy you. I've never done this before."

"You haven't?"

"No."

She gave a little laugh and pushed at him so she rolled onto the top. She smiled down at him, realizing he felt insecure and maybe a little embarrassed. "Well, I've never done this either…Don't worry. We'll figure it out, and I've got nothing but time for you."

He gently put his hands on the back of her neck and brought her mouth down to his. He rolled her back under him, and it began. She began to be his. He became hers. And they both knew it. What was between them was the stuff of forever. Or would have been if he had longer than a few days left.

He splayed his fingers on her stomach under her shirt, and a cold warning shot through him, like a premonition. This joining would result in a child... He froze. She didn't even know what he was. He couldn't do this to her. He wasn't staying. He couldn't leave with even the possibility of her carrying his child, having to raise it alone. And what kind of child would it be? It would be part wizard, and the blood lock was built against wizard blood. Would the child even be able to survive under that?

He'd never felt a regret as deep as in that moment.

"Shreve, what's wrong?"

He pulled away from her "I'm sorry. We can't be together this way." He covered his face with his hands.

"Why? I don't understand."

"I've never turned away from something I wanted as much as I want you. But you don't know what I am."

She sat up. "You're a Halfling," she said it confidently. "It doesn't matter to me."

"No. I wish I were a Halfling. I am a mix, that's true, but an unnatural one. I'm a clone."

Her eyes widened. "A clone..."

"I'm the genetic copy of a monster. I have my own mind, my own heart. I'm not the person he was spiritually, but I am exactly the same physically."

She looked down at her hands, her brow creasing. "Whose clone are you?"

"Copernicus."

Her mouth formed an O. He watched her process it. He waited in silence.

Her eyes came up and pinned him. A serious fire burned behind her gaze. "I know you, Shreve. Right there." She pointed at his chest. "You."

"Sabra, I…"

"No! I see you retreating from me. You can't tell me how to feel about this. You don't decide how I love, or what will make me stop. I decide the risks I take. I watched you die this morning, and then I watched you die again in my sleep. That forced the truth on me. The truth in my heart that I wanted to ignore. But now, I have no doubts about the way I feel about you. Does this revelation about your origins suck, yeah it does… Are you mine or not?"

"I'm yours."

"Then I don't want to hear about it again, unless it's somehow pertinent."

She moved toward him again, but he backed away and strode outside.

"Hey," she complained, following him out.

"I can't make love to you, Sabra."

She came up behind him and wrapped her arms around his torso, resting her cheek against his shoulder blade. "Why?"

"What if there's a child? I wasn't born, *I was created*. Copernicus wasn't born. He was a lab experiment."

"But—"

"I'm part wizard, Sabra! Those that cloned me added in their own genetic makeup just because they could. And now the wizards are threatening Regia. A blood lock is being created to hold them out. I have no idea if a wizard could live under that magic. You and I cannot risk creating life."

Her hold tightened, and her chest began to tremble against his back. He turned to face her. She looked up at him through a sheen of tears. "I'm so sorry." She shook her head back and forth. "So cruel... So unfair... What they did to you... I'll take whatever you can give me, however fragmented."

"My heart is yours. Every one of its broken pieces are yours."

She pulled free, turned, and walked away from him. She wrapped her arms around herself.

"What are you doing?" he asked quietly.

"This is a day of mourning. The sorrow has held steady since the dawn and taken many forms. If I am to move past losing a physical relationship with you, I have to mourn the loss of it first." She sighed deeply. "It would have been amazing, epic. I know it."

"You're quite astute at torturing me...I have something important to tell you, but if you need to be alone for a while..."

She turned on her heel and marched back to him. "Tell me. I need the distraction."

"The bodies have been found. Everyone is afraid and shaken by it. Four of those bastards were going to fight in the tournament, and it's believed they were killed because of that, or the fight began for that reason, even though the presence of Asher is confusing to them. There are only three names left on the list, someone named Urhal, Gahu, and you. The date for the tournament has been moved up in case what happened today is the work of someone trying to change the outcome."

"Moved up to when?"

"Tomorrow."

He framed her face with his hands. "What do you say? Are you ready to lead your people?"

"Yes...I'm ready."

"There's more. I listened to the women talking. They were upset when they learned you ran away, but it was good for them. Those I heard talking are ready to fight with you against the cultural norms."

He eyes lit up. "Really?"

"Really...oh, and Gahu and your brother are planning to search for you. Gahu says he's going to lock you in the underground until he breaks you."

She closed her eyes.

"Sabra?"

She wound her arms around his waist.

"What is it?" he asked.

"You. I love you. You don't want to break me. You don't treat me like I can't do anything on my own."

He snorted. "I think you're more capable than I am."

"No. I'm not. I can't open portals or heal myself instantly from mortal wounds. But still, you didn't even flinch when Silhon had a knife to my throat. You knew I could take him, didn't you?"

"I knew it."

"My strength doesn't threaten yours or lessen yours. I could never want someone who had to push me down to make themselves feel bigger...and I could never feel desire for a weakling. There's no one like you, Shreve."

He kissed her slowly. Marveling at who she was and that nothing he'd said had turned her away from him. Her love was real. He felt her physical response and forced himself to pull away.

"When do you think they will begin searching for me?"

"I don't know. I hope the tournament being moved up will put the idea out of their minds for a while, but maybe they are looking for you already."

"Let's get out of sight, then."

It was hard to be inside with her. So close. He wanted all of her, so much, every inch of his body hurt with wanting.

"Tell me everything, Shreve. Everything about you."

"Please don't ask that of me. You know I was bad. I don't want to relive all that."

She paced back and forth. He could feel her agitation in the air around her. "There has to be something we can do..."

"What?"

She stopped pacing and pinned him again with her eyes. "I want to feel you. I want to connect with you..." She rubbed her palms on her forearms. "It hurts...everything on me aches for you."

"It's the same for me."

She moved forward into his space. "Touch me."

"How?"

"I don't care. Just touch me."

He reached out and grasped both her forearms, just under the elbow. She closed her eyes and exhaled. He moved his hands up to her biceps as she reached out and put her hands on his face. She ran her fingers softly down the sides of his neck. He pulled her closer, moving his hands down to her waist, and then slid them up the back of her shirt until they rested flat on her shoulder blades.

Her skin was intoxicating and magnetic to his. It eased the frustration—and created new ones at the same time. But the sensation and ecstasy it brought just to touch her was worth the price of the pain it simultaneously created.

"Kiss me," she whispered.

"I'm afraid to."

"Don't be. If that's all we can have, I want it. When the moon rises, we'll run together, as we did the very first night, as wolves. Just one hour, Shreve. Hold me next to you and make love to my mouth with your own. Close your eyes and just imagine all the rest any way you want it."

He obeyed. In the breadth of a single hour, he knew torture as he never had...and it was exquisite.

When the moon crested the sky, they emerged into the cool night air. They shifted down into wolf form at the same time and took off running. Neither of them had ever run so hard, pushing their bodies to burn off the fire inside. Their spirits reached out and connected, allowing them to fully feel the depth of love the other had.

Shreve stored every moment in his heart. He had her. Her heart was his. Not because he took it, but because she gave it.

CHAPTER SIXTEEN

Tesla sat still while Rahaxeris pulled the painful surplus of magic from her hands. He took more time than usual, attempting to drain them down to nothing. When her fingers relaxed, he sat down across from her.

"Why do you want it the cube?" he asked.

It needs improvement. I can make it better. She signed.

"Merhl is making it better."

How does he know what to do?

"Maybe it's time you met him. He's like you in a number of ways."

How?

"He's gifted. His magic pools in his hands as well and causes him great pain. The more he creates, the less his hands hurt. Would you like to meet him? He's here."

She nodded enthusiastically. He stood and gestured for her to follow.

Merhl was in Rahaxeris' old lab. He looked up from the operating table where the cube sat, glowing blue, and smiled at Tesla. She rushed forward to the table.

"Don't touch!" Rahaxeris ordered her.

She scowled but put her hands behind her back and leaned in to look at it. She walked all the way around the table and then took a step back and looked up at her grandfather and the Ogre next to him.

"Manners?" Rahaxeris asked sternly.

It's nice to meet you, Merhl. She signed. *I like your hands. Grandpa told me about them. What do you think of mine?*

Rahaxeris translated what she said to Merhl.

"It's an honor to meet you, Tesla. Your hands are beautiful. Would you give me a closer look?"

She came closer and held her hands out for him. He touched her skin with one of his gnarled index fingers. Her power snapped on his fingertip. She pulled her hands back, embarrassed. He shocked her by laughing.

"Don't worry," Merhl assured her. "It took me a long time to learn control over my gifts. You'll learn to make it do what you want. You didn't hurt me. It kind of tickled."

I like you. I think we can teach each other some things.

Again, Rahaxeris translated.

"What can you teach me?" Merhl asked.

I can show you what you're doing wrong with that cube. You haven't even activated the heart of the second interior. Did you not see it?

There was an awkward silence after Rahaxeris told Merhl what she signed. Merhl looked between her and the cube, twice, his brow furrowed. "Are you sure that's what she said?"

"Quite. Do you know what she's talking about?"

"No, I mean I do, but there is no second interior, let alone a heart."

Tesla began signing at top speed, her eyes bright. *He can't see it! It will work, but it won't work very well, if the heart isn't activated. You need to let me handle this!*

Rahaxeris didn't translate this time. "I want to trust you, but how do I know you really know what you're talking about? There's too much riding on this. I need proof first."

She wrung her hands and cast her eyes around the room. She grabbed Merhl's notes from the side of the table. He had an intricate x-ray type sketch of the cube on the top page. She laid the paper in front of her and slapped her hand flat over the drawing. Snaking red electric snaps hit the paper all around her hand.

She pulled her hand away and held the drawing up for them to see. The sketch lifted off the paper like a 3-D hologram. She touched it lightly with her index finger, and it opened a layer that Merhl had never drawn. She pointed to a small line and then flicked it with her finger and thumb. It broke open, showing them the heart of the second interior.

The color drained from Merhl's face. "How could I have missed that?" He picked up the cube and made to hand it to Tesla.

Rahaxeris grabbed his wrist. She looked furiously at him.

"I need more, Tesla. Just a bit more."

Her hands lit up. He recognized the motion, but before he could reach to stop her, she put her hands on her chest, filling the air with a fog of electricity.

"Stop, Tesla! No!" he shouted.

"What is this?" Merhl asked.

"She's aging herself."

"What?"

"Help me!"

He put his hands on the barrier around her, Merhl followed his example. They pushed a hole through it, and the fog vanished in an electric snap. Tesla lay on the floor, twice as tall as she had been. Now she resembled a twelve-year-old.

Her eyes snapped open when her grandfather touched her.

"Why?" he shouted at her. "Almost your whole childhood is gone now! Just because you're impatient to be taken seriously."

She stood and stretched her arms, looking down at herself, completely composed and seemingly indifferent to her grandfather's anger. Her clothes were torn and scorched. Again, her beauty had grown with her. She pulled her feet out of her torn shoes.

"Merhl, please get some clothes for her from the closet over there. I think there's a spare lab coat."

Merhl rushed over with the lab coat, catching a glimpse of the top of the red flower shape over her heart. He gaped at her.

She looked back at him questioningly. He pointed at it.

"What else can you do?"

She smiled and walked a few steps away from her grandfather. She reached down, grabbed the edge of nothing, and tore it open. Merhl could see the ripple in the air, and then she vanished behind it like a curtain.

Rahaxeris rolled his eyes and threw up his hands in exasperation. "Oh great. She's a world jumper."

"Do you know what this means?" Merhl asked.

"Yeah. Forest is going to kill me... Can you see where she went?"

Merhl walked over to the invisible tear and looked at it closely. "Clever girl," he murmured. "She went to Polyhedron. She didn't even break the strata, she just slid through it."

Rahaxeris ground his teeth together. "I'll give her three minutes, then I'm going after her."

Merhl chuckled. "Didn't realize you'd enjoy being a grandfather this much? You've got your hands full."

"Yeah. I realize the benefits of not being a family man, only after it's too late."

The air shivered, and Tesla stepped back into the room, her hair windblown. She was holding a small grey cube in the palm of her hand, a triumphant look on her face. She put it down on the table next to the other one.

This cube is not the same, but I will show you what I can do with it. She signed adamantly. *After Merhl looks it over and discovers all he can about it.*

Rahaxeris sighed and crossed his arms, translating to Merhl.

Merhl looked the cube over once before opening its seamless exterior skin. He couldn't see the purpose of this cube, but he turned it on, twisting its core in a full circle. Blue light began glowing in the corners. Green characters pulsed on the sides. Merhl's fingers stilled. He pulled his hands back and wrapped the cube in a bubble of energy.

He looked at Rahaxeris. "It's a bomb."

"Are you sure?"

"Yes!"

"Tesla! Did you know that's what that was?"

She nodded nonchalantly.

The cube exploded inside the bubble.

"What did that prove?" Rahaxeris demanded.

She walked over to the table and popped the energy bubble with her fingertip as easily as if it were a soap bubble. Smoke and broken machine parts fell out. She flexed her fingers and began reassembling the cube. In less than thirty seconds, it was back together, unburned, and seemingly unused. She held it up for them to see. Then the cube levitated off her palm and dangled in the air over her hand. A lightning snake emerged from the center of her palm and slithered through the skin of the cube. The red light ran a circuit, twisting up from the bottom to the top, and then vanished. She handed the cube back to Merhl.

What can you see now?

Rahaxeris crowded next to Merhl, desperate to see, as he opened the cube again. The whole interior was different than before. Merhl touched it in a few places, but he realized quickly what she'd done, and he closed it again before he activated it.

"Well?" Rahaxeris demanded.

Merhl gaped at Tesla. He gave her a little bow before turning to Rahaxeris. "Not only did she repair it, remake it actually, she turned it into a weapon ten times as strong as it had been originally...I don't want to relinquish the work on the tesseract to her, but I need her help." He turned back to her. "I certainly mean you no disrespect, but..."

She smiled and shook her head. *You're right. I need to help you. I am not an Ogre. I cannot create a blood lock. But I can help make it stronger.*

Rahaxeris translated.

"I'll learn sign language before you come back, miss."

She looked down and made a strange noise. She huffed and tried again to speak. Her cheeks heated, and she looked on the verge of tears. *I thought I'd grow out of this. I want to talk so badly.*

"I'm sorry, sweetheart." Rahaxeris said. "Let's get you home. And please, tell your mother your current age was all your doing and not any fault of mine."

CHAPTER SEVENTEEN

Shreve awoke suddenly in the middle of the night. Sabra was sleeping soundly, her back nestled against his chest, her head on his arm. It was heaven and hell at the same time. He ran his hand softly up and down her arm. Why was he awake? His pulse hiccupped, choking the air in his lungs. His mortality was slapping him in the face. His heart stammered. Not long now. He just needed a few more days. That was all, just a few more. His pulse righted, but it was weaker than ever.

He tucked her hair behind her ear and kissed the side of her neck once. The dawn would bring the end of this dream he'd had of her. The tournament would end everything. If she won, *when* she won, she would be the new leader. Her people would need her. They would absorb her. She couldn't be seen with him. She'd have no time for him. And he had no time left. He couldn't afford to die out here. His blood was too important. He had to deliver it.

He wrapped his arm around her and pulled her closer. He had to tell her goodbye. He thought about the morning he'd first realized he was dying. He'd found what he was looking for. He'd found forgiveness. He'd found his face and his family. And he'd found Sabra. He loved her, and she loved him. He hadn't expected to have even one of those things.

She sighed in her sleep and turned over, facing him. Hours passed like mere minutes while he gazed at her.

****

Sabra woke up alone. She was instantly alert. "Shreve?"

No answer. She got up and rushed outside. She almost collided into him. "Oh! There you are."

"I've been to the Lair. The arena is all set. The tournament will begin soon. I've only just enough time to teach you something

191

important."

"Okay." She tried to sound steadier than she felt. "Will you kiss me good morning first?"

He smiled and gathered her into his arms. "Good morning." He pressed his lips so gently against hers. She pressed back harder. His touch was so sweet, but she could detect sorrow behind it.

"I never got a chance to take your other opponent's measure, but I fear Gahu is going to be very dangerous today. When you show up, it's going to slap at his already hurt ego. He already wants to make you pay for the humiliation you've caused him. He thinks this is his day to take power… When you show up, ready to fight him, he's going to want to make an example of his dominance with you. It's beyond personal."

"I'm sure you're right. What are you going to teach me?"

"If you are disarmed, you will lose your edge and be at a disadvantage. You need to call out the beast if that happens."

"But I asked Asher about that before. He said it would take too long to shift."

"Just shift your hands. Run from your opponent if you have to, to have enough time."

"I've never tried anything like that," she admitted.

"Try it now. We don't have much time."

She held her hands out and tried. As she feared, her whole body shifted, elongated and brutal. She pulled it back. "Sorry. I know that's hideous. Please try and forget it."

"Shut up and try again. Focus and don't worry what you look like."

Again she shifted her whole body. "I don't know where to begin."

"Close your eyes," he ordered, taking her hands in his. "Feel your bones. Think of Gahu, what he wants to do to you. All you have is your hands. Make him pay. Show him the type of woman you are."

She listened to his voice and envisioned the fight ahead. But it wasn't Gahu, and what he had or would do to her that forced her hands. She thought of her mother and grandmother. She thought of the women locked in the underground, chained, beaten, and raped daily, because they had somehow displeased their men. She thought of Tucker and how he'd lost his identity under this macho ideology.

"Call it out, Sabra. Now!"

Heat shivered down her arms to her fingers.

"That's it! Keep going!"

Her hatred of injustice lit her bones on fire as they stretched, her fingernails lengthening and hardening into claws.

"Look, you did it."

Sabra opened her eyes. Only her hands were in beast form. "But it took so long. Even if I ran and evaded, it would take too long."

"Turn your palms up."

He placed his hands over her beastly ones "What are you doing?" she asked.

He jerked his hands back, so her claws raked and cut his hands.

"There. Now you won't have to worry about it. My blood is under your fingernails. You just needed to do it once. If you need to do it again, it will be easy."

She curled her monster hands and let them shrink back to normal. "Thank you."

He shook his head. "It's time for you to get ready. I'll be watching you fight. You won't see me though."

"Because you'll be invisible?"

"Yes...I have to tell you goodbye now."

"Why? It won't take me that long to get there. I'll win, and I'll see you after. I'll tell everyone that you're my man. I'll be the leader. They won't have a choice but to accept you. And you won't have to stay out here in hiding. You'll come live with me, at the very top of the mountain."

"It's a beautiful dream. One I'll take with me. I'd give anything to have it come true."

"It will," she said decisively. "It's not a dream. It will be reality in a few hours."

"There's no future for us."

Hurt and anger mixed inside her. "You're wrong! Why would you say that?! Because you can't give me children?"

"I'm dying. I have to tell you goodbye."

Her battered heart tore like fabric. "You're dying." She tried the words; they were bitter in her mouth. "How could you be dying?"

"I've been dying since before I met you. My DNA is deteriorating. I'm all worn out inside. I've not got long left."

"But...but... If you're dying... Why...why would you leave me? Why would you rob me of whatever time is left?"

"There's almost none."

"No!" She pushed him with both of her hands. "How could you abandon me like this? How?"

He grabbed her and held her as she swung at him. She hit him once in the chest as she cried out.

"Sabra, I have no choice. I want to live. Do you really think I would choose to leave you?" He tipped her chin up and kissed her. "I would never leave you. I love you."

"Then stay. I don't care about the tournament anymore, not if it takes our time away, not even one hour, or even one minute. Let me have every second. I don't care about anything else."

He shook his head sadly. "You have to build your own future with your capable hands and your indestructible heart. I have to give the last of my life for the blood lock that will protect the world."

"You're going to give your life for *them*?" She was furious.

"No. Not for them. For you. You have to live, Sabra. Promise me you will, and that you'll thrive, and maybe from time to time you'll remember me and that I loved you." He touched the tear on her cheek. It clung to his fingertip. He curled his hand into a fist, her tear encased inside it. "That's mine. It will go with me."

"Shreve, please," she begged. "*Please.*" But it was no good.

"I'll watch you fight. Then I'll be gone."

Something inside her snapped. She was thrust into a reality she couldn't change. Her heart locked down, her mind focused sharply. He was leaving her, and she couldn't make him stay. The tournament lay at her feet, and she'd never been so ready to kill. She pushed past him, back into the hidden dwelling. He followed. She went for her knapsack. He watched in silence as she stripped down and dressed for the fight. The dark clothes clung and moved like a second skin. She laced her boots tightly and braided her hair back. Last was her belt, connected to her scabbard. She held it out to him.

He came forward and took it, wrapping it around her waist and fastening the buckle. He picked her sword up and slid it into the sheath. Slowly, he coiled her whip and fastened it to her other hip. He put his index finger in his mouth and bit down on his fingertip. He held his bleeding finger up next to her face.

"Close your eyes, Valkyrie," he whispered.

He drew lines on her face with his finger. Ancient symbols of power and death. His blood was her war paint. There was an inferno inside her. She'd never felt anything like it. The blood pulled on her skin as it dried. She grabbed him and held on with all her might before kissing him goodbye.

"You watch. I'm going to fight for you. You'll be proud of me. I'm going to win. And every day after, I'll live for you. I'm never letting you go. There'll never be anyone for me, but you. Never."

"I'll watch you. And then I'll come back to haunt you."

She kissed him again with all the passion of the fire inside her. "You better come back to haunt me. I told you where I'll be. Don't get lost."

"Go, Sabra. Claim your destiny."

"I'll love you forever, Shreve."

"And I you... Forever."

She ran from him while she could, out and through the trees, sticking to the paths. She kept her eyes forward, burning brighter and hotter with every step. Anyone in her way would die. Her opponents would die. Shreve was watching her. She'd fight with her whole heart.

CHAPTER EIGHTEEN

She heard the crowd before she saw them. Everyone gathered around the main square but not in it. It had been roped off. Urhal and Gahu were already standing in the center. Samuel stood on the speaking boulder, over the crowd, shouting about the glory of their traditions and how they all hastened to have a new leader.

She pushed through the people. They parted and whispered as she passed. She didn't hesitate when she reached the rope, she just ducked under it and walked to the center, head held high. She could feel Gahu's murderous gaze on her, but she didn't bother looking at him.

Samuel looked down at her, halting in his speech. She stared at him defiantly. He cleared his throat and looked away from her. "Our third champion has arrived."

All the men in the crowd jeered at her. She didn't bat an eye.

"As is custom, the fighters will be in order, from lowest to highest rank. Sabra and Urhal will fight first. The victor will fight Gahu. Whoever lives is the champion and will be the new pack leader. Let the tournament begin."

The people roared and cheered. Gahu made to leave the arena, but he stopped next to her for a moment.

"If you survive this round, you'll wish you hadn't," he said quietly, so only she could hear.

She smiled at him. "No, if I survive this round, *you'll* wish I hadn't."

Rage burned in his eyes. "You look disgusting. What's on your face?"

Her smile broadened. "The blood of my lover... Now back off. You have to wait your turn."

With everyone's eyes on him, he had no choice but to leave the arena.

Huge, muscled, and menacing, Urhal faced her from the other side of the square. In order to beat him, she'd have to be faster and fight dirtier. His weapons of choice were an axe and a longsword. The sun glinted off the metal as he brandished the axe first. She unhooked her whip and let the thong fall loose. He growled at her, baring his teeth. In response, she cracked her whip so loudly that many in the crowd jumped in alarm and covered their ears.

"Fight!" Samuel yelled.

She moved forward, raising her arm again. She'd expected him to hold on to his weapon, but she miscalculated. Urhal's axe came flying across the arena at her. She moved to the side, but the blade clipped the side of her arm. He ran toward her.

She lashed out. The hooked tip of her whip snapped into Urhal's eye and tore it out as she pulled back. As he yelled and held his face, she ran and slid next to him and out of his sight. He tried to look around as he drew his longsword. Coming up behind him, drawing her katana, she sliced deep into the soft place behind both of his knees in one fluid move.

He fell back, his legs now unable to hold up his weight. He thrust his sword clumsily at her from the ground. She kicked the sword from his grasp and caught it. She jumped onto his chest and stabbed clean through his hand, pinning him to the ground with his own sword. Crouching down, she held her katana to his throat.

"No! Please!" A terrified plea reflected in his eyes.

She flinched. "Do you yield?"

"Yes! Yes, I yield!"

She stood up and looked at Samuel. "I win."

When he scowled, she turned to the crowd. "Say it again, Urhal!"

"Sabra wins!" he shouted.

"Did you all hear him?" she demanded.

Half of the crowd booed, but the rest, the women mostly, began chanting, *Sabra won! Sabra won!*

She turned back to Samuel. "There's no need for me to kill him. The match is mine."

He crossed his arms over his chest. "All right," he said slowly. "Prepare for your next match."

She moved to the edge of the arena, sheathed her sword, and recoiled her whip. Urhal was lifted and taken away. She touched her arm gently, testing the severity of the wound. Blood saturated her sleeve all the way down to her wrist. She sighed, feeling the chill creep into her arm as she continued to lose blood.

Sabra leaned against the ropes, the crowd pressing in behind her. There was too much congestion, people packed in too closely, that no one noticed what happened to her. Her breath caught as she felt Shreve touch her shoulders. Still invisible, he tied a strip of cloth around her arm. He said nothing, pressed a kiss against her temple, and absorbed back into the crowd.

Gahu came into the arena and faced her from the other side. *Now the hard part.*

His weapons of choice were a broadsword and a mace. She felt the lingering trace of Shreve's kiss on her temple. He was watching, she reminded herself. She would make him proud. She would win this for him.

"I'll have no mercy on you, bitch," he yelled. "You're going to die. The pack could never be led by a traitorous whore like you."

The men in the crowd cheered at his statement.

"You'll be begging for my mercy, Gahu. I guess we'll see if I give it."

"Enough!" Samuel yelled. "Fight!"

He charged instantly. Everything slowed for her. She stepped forward, the whip spiraling around her body as she spun in a circle and then rolled her arm out in a snap. The whip uncoiled in the distance between them. The end wrapped three times around his neck, the shards in the leather biting into his flesh. She pulled the handle with both hands as hard as she could. He went down on his knees, dropping his mace and pulling his sword. In a downward strike, he cut the whip with his sword, the end of it still clinging around his neck like a constricting snake. He quickly unwound it.

She ran full force into him, before he could get off his knees, knocking him onto his back. She tried to dart away, but he grabbed her ankle, pulling her down, dragging her back to him. His sword flashed through the air. She grabbed his wrist with both of her hands. They strained against each other, pushing. He brought his hand up and grabbed the wound on her arm. She cried out as he dug in his fingers. The pain caused her grip to slacken, and he yanked his sword hand free of her grasp.

Her leg got twisted wrong under him as he rolled to get up. He tackled her flat on the ground under him, knocking the air from her lungs and pinning her arms straight down between them. He snarled in her face. She remembered her first training session with Asher and the advice he'd given her that day. She stretched her hands down a little farther and grabbed Gahu's crotch, digging in her nails.

He cried out and scrambled to get out of her hold. She clung as they rolled over and over. He was pale and out of breath, flat on his back. She turned to the side, grabbed his arm, and wrapped her legs across his upper body. Crossing her ankles by his head, she pulled his arm down, breaking it over her thigh.

She let go and rolled away from him as soon as she felt the bone snap. He lumbered to his feet, his broken arm hanging uselessly, his sword in his other hand.

She pulled her katana and brandished it at him. He blocked her strike, and she knew instantly that he was a better swordsman than she was. They circled each other. She thrust at him, but he wound his sword in a circle around hers, the metal sliding together. With a perfect twist of his wrist, her sword flew out of her hand.

"Now, you die," he said smugly.

He swung his sword at her in a wide sideways arc. She ducked it, rolled past his legs, and jumped up behind him. She reached over the top of his head as her hands stretched out into beast form. She hooked her claws into his eyes and pulled him straight down to the ground. Blinded, he let go of his sword, his body going limp. Sabra jumped onto his chest and wrapped her viscous hands around his throat. She allowed him to breathe, the pressure she applied more of a threat.

"Say it, Gahu. Tell everyone I won. Tell me you yield."

Silence fell over the crowd. Everyone held their breath.

"Live or die?" Her claws bore down.

"I'd rather die than submit to a woman," he wheezed.

His unbroken arm came up, and he grabbed her hair, yanking her head back. Her talons sank through his neck. Gahu choked to death on his own blood.

She stood, blood dripping from her hands, looking out at the crowd, the shock on their faces mirroring her own. Samuel came up beside her, bent down and touched the ground next to her foot. Everyone followed his lead, bowing to her and touching the ground.

"Well done," Shreve whispered in her ear.

She held still and closed her eyes as the man she loved enveloped her in his invisible arms. She breathed him in, feeling his hair against her cheek.

"I will love you always, Sabra." He kissed her forehead, her cheeks, and very briefly her mouth, before releasing her. "Farewell."

She was a statue; she felt as if her soul left her body, taken away with his.

Everyone stood upright again and waited for her to speak, to act.

I did it. I really did it.

She swallowed. "Today will be a day of mourning... For Asher." She had no other words. She picked up Gahu's mace and strode toward the entrance of the mountain. The people followed, murmuring. She ignored them. She entered the mountain and went straight for the tunnel leading down to the underground.

There were five women chained in cells down there. Using the mace, she broke open every cell door.

"Unlock their chains," she ordered the guard and then turned to face those watching her. "This disgraceful practice is over!" she shouted. "As are many more that have become common place. Go to your homes and finish the day in mourning. Tomorrow, things will be clearer. Tomorrow, I will show you the new direction of our culture. Go now."

The crowd funneled out until, finally, she was alone. Sabra's heart hammered painfully against her ribs as she left the underground and climbed the stairs, past the door of her old home, all the way up to the top. Two guards stood on either side of the double doors. She nodded at them and pushed the doors open.

She bolted the doors behind her and stood in the center of the vast, stone room that had been empty since Philippe died. To get through it all, she'd held herself perfectly still inside. But now it all broke loose. She sank to the floor, shaking. After Sophie was killed, she'd believed it was impossible to cry harder than that, but at that moment, she proved herself wrong.

Sabra broke into fragments as she felt everything. She'd won the tournament! That was disbelief and ecstatic joy. She'd lost everyone, her parents, her siblings, and Asher. That was bitter grief and loneliness. She was in love. That was life and oxygen and soul fire.

Shreve. She said his name over and over, swallowed whole in the anguish of losing him.

****

Shreve watched her as she broke open the cells, feeling pride, and knowing she would be all right. When she sent everyone away, he was the last to go. He could have touched her again. He could have kissed her and told her how much he loved her, but he had already done that. She would have clung to him, and he would have lost his will to go.

He walked through the Lair and out, only dropping his invisibility once he reached the wilds. His pulse fluttered unevenly, and he gasped as needles of pain shot through his heart and flowed through his veins. *Not yet! Not here!*

He had to get to Kyhael as soon as possible. He wasn't going to make it if he walked. It was the last of his power, the very last drop, he used to open a portal.

CHAPTER NINETEEN

Rahaxeris, Merhl, and Tesla all sat around the cube, working on it. To Rahaxeris, she was calm that morning, seemingly pleased that she was there and a part of the process. Merhl was as good as his word and had learned sign language, or enough that he could understand most of what Tesla said.

All of a sudden she grabbed Rahaxeris by the arm, shocking him with her hand. Her eyes were huge and urgent.

"What?"

Shreve is here! Come on! She signed at top speed.

She jumped up from her chair and bolted from the room. He got up and rushed after her into the main chamber. Shreve was lying on the floor. He looked dead. Rahaxeris picked him up and hefted him to the lab, where he laid him on the operating table. Rahaxeris checked his pulse. He was on the edge.

Closing his eyes, Rahaxeris put his hands flat on Shreve's chest. He exhaled, sending a wave of power into his body.

Shreve gasped and opened his eyes. "I made it...I made it," he rasped.

"What happened to you?"

"Out...of time. You have to take my blood now."

Rahaxeris allowed himself only one second to feel, then he gathered his instruments for the extraction. Tesla stood next to the table and took Shreve's hand. He glanced at her for a moment, then his eyes rolled back, and he fell unconscious.

Rahaxeris came back to the table, tore open Shreve's shirt, and swiftly cut open his chest with a long scalpel. He grabbed another instrument with many points, about to insert the end into Shreve's heart when Tesla ran around to him and knocked the instrument out of his hand.

Are you crazy? She signed. *That's not right!*

"Tesla, I know what I'm doing. I have to separate all the strands of DNA in his blood."

You're going to kill him!

"I don't have time to argue with you! He's almost dead already. He knew he was giving his life for this. I can't save him."

Maybe you can't, old man, but I can.

"Tesla...you don't..."

Are we back to that, Grandfather? Remember the cube? I can get what we need for the blood lock and save his life.

"How?"

She smiled. *Just watch.*

"Don't call me old man," he grumbled.

She put her hands inside Shreve's chest and operated on him with nothing but her fingers. The red light in her hands extended beyond her skin, stretching and twisting, slicing, or pulling as was needed. She combed through his blood, separating all the parts and races like shafts of hair through a comb. She grabbed a vial, tipped it into the stream, and handed the elixir of Regia's salvation to her grandfather.

Shreve was submerged in the darkest currents of death sleep. She didn't know if he could ever be roused, but she didn't tell Rahaxeris that she had even a shred of self-doubt. She would have liked to ask Shreve his opinion at that moment, but she had no choice but to select one race for him and discard the others.

So much of him was taken away. When she closed him back up, his life still hung in the balance. His fate now rested in his own will.

****

In the middle of the night, after an entire day of pouring their talent and magic, along with Shreve's distilled blood, into the tesseract, Rahaxeris, Merhl, and Tesla all sat back, exhausted. Merhl closed the cube, now glowing a vibrant red. The blood lock was ready. It wouldn't be active until Journey placed it inside the flames of the Heart and Tesla turned it on.

CHAPTER TWENTY

Sabra braced her hands on the railing of her balcony and watched the evening sky dance. After being the leader of the pack for only a week, she'd learned that her gut had been right all along. This was the work she was meant for. It was wonderful and exhausting, and there was already a sense of hope building in the people. There was still much that had to heal, and she recognized it would take considerable time. But time was all she had.

She threw herself fully into the work, giving her people all of her strength, energy, and mind. But now the day was ending. She looked out from the lofty place over the land. It was an amazing view, one she would never share with anyone. She knew bitterly that her life would be solitary. Only when she was alone did she allow her tears to flow freely, as they did at that moment.

She was waiting for him. He'd said he would come back to haunt her. He was late.

The air was thin and cold around her. She went inside and closed the balcony doors. Her new place was most agreeable, since she'd cleaned out all of Philippe's stuff. The pelts he'd used to wear on his cloak and the ones that were used as rugs and blankets, she'd taken down to the square the morning after the tournament. The dead were identified and claimed by their family members and given proper funeral rights.

She didn't see the need in replacing the furniture. The massive bed was terribly comfortable now that she had new bedding for it. But again, despite the softness, its size made her feel alone and adrift at night.

Tucker had tried to reach out to her. Since she refused to see him, he sent letters of apology, passed to her by her guards. He seemed sincere. She just wasn't ready to let him back in her life. Not yet. She sat down at her desk with the dinner plate that had been brought in earlier and began reading over the requests the people were starting to send her.

A knock sounded on her doors. She got up and walked over to them, about to gently give her guards a piece of her mind. It better be urgent, whatever it was, because it was well past the time she allowed anyone to reach her, and they knew it.

"What is it?" she asked through the door.

There was no answer. Annoyed, she pulled the long sliding bolt to the side and opened the door. "This better be impor—"

Her eyes dilated, fire and storm burning through them. The force of an explosion hit her in the chest, and she was thrown backward. The fire storm in her eyes filled her whole head and then spread through her extremities. It burned for one second of agony and then turned to a bright ecstasy. The force pulled her to him. Invisible, immortal cords of light and heat tied them together. Hands, hearts, lungs, eyes, and souls all bound.

"What just happened?" She was breathless.

Shreve was trying to catch his breath as well. "If I'm not mistaken, I think you're my destined life mate."

She shook her head, trembling. "Makes no sense... You're dead."

He took her mouth, hot and hard, stealing the little bit of breath she had. "Do I feel like a ghost to you?"

"Not at all. But how can we be destined life mates? After all the contact we've had before?"

He smiled. "Look closely at me. Do I seem different to you?"

She looked. He was different. His face was close, very close to what it had been, but he was, unbelievably, even more beautiful than before. The green of his eyes was clearer, as if his spirit had been cleansed and the past purged from him.

"Perhaps, some of it was there before. A trace. When we ran

together?" she asked.

"Maybe. I feel as though I have never truly been me, until now. I am changed. I'm healthy now, with a long life ahead of me. I am no longer mixed. My blood has been purified. I am only a shifter now and nothing else."

She framed his face, adjusting to the slight difference in his appearance. "If you're a shifter, and you're my destined life mate, then this is your true face, Shreve."

A single tear slid down his cheek. "I suppose that's right. This is my true face."

She pressed her lips against his tear. "I always saw you."

She dragged him inside and bolted the doors. They wound around each other, the ties that bound them pulling tighter until there was nothing between them. They demolished each other's innocence of physical love throughout the night, using every inch of the considerable real estate of the bed, vast areas of the floor, and even out on the balcony, *brazenly* under the moon.

One Month Later...

The evening was pleasantly warm. Shreve kissed Sabra's hand. "You look beautiful tonight."

She ignored his compliment as though she hadn't heard it. "Do I look nervous? It's obvious, isn't it?"

"What are you nervous about?"

"What if your family doesn't like me?" She fidgeted and smoothed her skirt for the fifth time in a row.

"They would have no reason to not like you," he said pragmatically. "If they accept me, after everything I put them through in my previous life, you've got nothing to worry about."

She blew out her breath as they entered through the gate into

Forest and Syrus' garden. "I still can't believe the Hailemarris is your sister."

"I think you'll like her. You two are quite alike, actually."

"I don't doubt I'll like *her*. I've admired her for so long. I'm just worried, when I actually meet her, I'll make a fool of myself by acting like a twelve-year-old fangirl."

He laughed and caught her up in his arms and kissed her mouth sweetly, until she rested easily against him.

"Relax."

She smiled. "Don't you know it's a bad idea to tell a woman to relax?"

He looked confused. "No. Why?"

She looked up at the cottage and didn't answer. "This is really where they live?"

"This is it."

"It's really...special. Charming."

"Yeah. It's quickly become one of my favorite places."

He squeezed her hand before knocking on the front door. A tall, and terribly handsome, vampire answered, giving them an easy smile.

"Shreve," Syrus said, shaking his hand, then he turned his grey eyes on her. "So this is Sabra?"

She felt her nerves bounce in her chest and could only nod as he shook her hand as well. "Pleasure to meet you," he said. "Come in."

Sabra smiled unconsciously as they walked into the house, reality making her a little dizzy. The ex-prince and most powerful mage in all Regia had just invited her in. She wasn't able to really absorb the warm charm of the living room before she was confronted by Forest.

Sabra stared at her. Strikingly beautiful, she looked much like

Shreve. They had the same eyes. Forest was like the finest sword, exquisitely detailed with a deadly sharp edge. She didn't shake Sabra's hand, but pulled her into a welcoming hug.

"Thank you for coming. I can't tell you how happy I am to meet you. Please make yourself at home."

She released Sabra and gave Shreve a hug as well.

"Where's my niece?" he asked.

"Dad has her. They'll be here in a little while. Come, sit down."

She ushered them to the couch. They sat, and Forest pinned Sabra with her eyes. "So, tell me all about yourself. I've heard about your impressive victory in the tournament."

"Yes. I didn't realize it at the time, but I guess I have you to thank for some of my success."

"Oh?"

"I used your sword. I hope you don't mind. Shreve gave it to me."

Forest looked at Shreve and smiled. "He did, did he? I was wondering what happened to that."

"I'm sorry. I didn't realize...I'll be happy to give it back," Sabra said quickly.

Forest waved her hand dismissively. "You keep it. I don't want it back."

"But surely you must. It's a very special blade. So unique and beautiful."

Forest smiled broadly. "Thank you for the compliment. I actually made that sword."

"Really?"

"Yes."

"I'll be sure to give it back as soon as possible."

Forest chuckled. "No. I seriously don't want it. I promise. You keep it."

"Why would you not want it?" Sabra was confused.

"Show her your new one," Shreve said to Forest. "Then she'll understand."

Forest got up and left the room as Syrus came in. He set a couple of wine-filled flutes on the short table in front of them.

"Here," he said. "Dinner is just about ready. Where did Forest go?"

"She's getting her freaky sword to show Sabra."

Syrus sat down. "Ah. Interested in weapons, Sabra?"

"As much as the next girl who grows up in a dumbass, misogynistic culture and has to kill to be taken seriously."

Syrus laughed appreciatively and gave Shreve a meaningful look. "You do realize our women are going to be fast friends, don't you?"

"Yeah. I've already thought of that."

Forest came back into the room with her sword. Sabra stood up, coming close to get a better look, in awe of the beauty and originality of it. She'd never seen a hilt that looked like a tree. Or a blade made from glass, let alone glass that held lightning inside it. The sword was a lethal work of art.

"Careful," Forest warned as she handed it to her. "It's deadly."

"I've never seen anything like it."

"It's one of a kind," Forest agreed.

Sabra looked at her. "Just like you. It suits you." She handed it back, and Forest slid it into its ornately carved wooden scabbard.

"Thank you."

"Let's eat," Syrus said.

The four of them sat down at the table and enjoyed a fantastic meal and each other's company. Sabra's nerves were all forgotten. Her heart became lighter than it had been in a very long time. She knew everything about Shreve now, and it made her so happy to watch the way he interacted with his sister. The ease and the trust between them was amazing, given how new their relationship was. It seemed like Forest needed him almost as much as he needed her.

Sabra sipped her wine when her plate was clean. "That was an amazing meal."

"I'm glad you enjoyed it," Syrus said.

Forest smiled into Sabra's eyes. "He's good at everything, but he really is superior in the kitchen."

"Lucky girl," Sabra said. Then she turned to Shreve. "Can you cook at all?"

"No. But why would I need to? You're the pack leader. Every time you've been hungry, I've seen you ring that bell and food appears."

"How are you settling into all that?" Forest asked.

"So well!" Sabra exclaimed. "And everyone is really accepting of Shreve."

"She may be over stating that," Shreve corrected. "But it's mostly true. I've only just decided that since I'm a shifter, I can do a good work by finding the shifters that were displaced by Aluka Circle and bringing them to the Lair."

"We want to rebuild the ties wolves and shifters used to have and open up our community to them as a first step to ending the mindset that wolves should live apart from the rest of Regia," Sabra said.

"That's an excellent plan. I'm going back to work next week for the first time since Tesla was born. We should confer on this in a professional capacity. Could you come by Fortress soon? Both of you?"

Sabra smiled brightly. "Yeah. Of course."

"Great!" Forest looked out of the window. "It's dark now," she said to Syrus.

He got up from the table. "I'll go make the fire."

"What's going on?" Sabra asked.

"Family initiation." Forest smiled. "It's time for s'mores."

When they were all outside, standing around the heat with wire pokers in the fire, a portal opened, and Rahaxeris and Tesla came through.

Sabra was spellbound by Tesla. It wasn't shocking that someone with such gorgeous parents was gorgeous as well, but aside from her beauty, she was so strange...exotic and frightening. The girl pinned her with her eyes, and there was an unmasked animosity there. She looked Sabra over thoroughly before running at Shreve and hugging him.

The two of them were thick as thieves. They signed animatedly at each other, and Shreve laughed at a few things she *said*. He redirected her attention back onto Sabra.

"Tesla, this is Sabra. My destined life mate. She's the leader of the werewolves."

Tesla signed something at her. The movements of her hands were abrupt, harsh even.

"Tesla!" Shreve chided.

"What did she say?" Sabra asked.

"She said, *If you hurt him, I'll make you pay*."

She would have laughed. She wanted to, but she could tell the girl was totally serious. "I'll remember that. But I would never hurt him. I promise."

Tesla narrowed her large grey eyes and crossed her arms over her chest, scrutinizing Sabra again, possibly even closer than before. Her face smoothed out, and she nodded once at Sabra before turning on her heel and striding into the house.

"I'm sorry," Forest said. "She's never acted like that before."

"No, no. That's fine." Sabra smirked, thoroughly amused. "Since she's not easily won over, I'll know when I really have her affection, if I ever do."

"After she saved my life, before I came back to you, she started treating me like her pet," Shreve said.

"She claimed you as her pet before that," Syrus said. "Remember the fuzzy blanket?"

The two men laughed.

"I'm going to go talk to her for a minute." Shreve went back into the house as Rahaxeris came up to Sabra.

"Welcome to the family," he said, taking one of her hands in his long sharp ones.

She swallowed, trying not to be afraid. He was the first *Rune-dy* she had ever seen. Shreve had told her about him, and not to be scared, but it was difficult. He took a step back from her and walked over to Forest. She handed him a poker and a marshmallow. Sabra's fear of him faded as he took the silly thing and put it in the fire.

She smiled bemusedly, her heart lifting again. She had a new family. A mate, a sister, a brother, a father, and even a temperamental tween niece. Life felt pleasantly full.

****

"What's wrong, Tesla? Why were you rude like that?" Shreve asked.

Sorry. She signed. *I shouldn't have acted like that. She's very beautiful. I'll be better the next time I see her. Do you think she hates me?*

"Of course she doesn't hate you. Just give her a chance—you'll like her."

I just kind of liked having you to myself, but once she has the baby, you won't have time for me.

"Baby?"

Tesla rolled her eyes and made a little snorting sound. *I saw it inside her. The embryo is only a few hours old. A girl.*

Shreve felt dizzy. He and Sabra *had* made love a few hours ago. He tried to focus his attention back on Tesla.

"No matter how many children I may have, there will only ever be one of you. You saved my life. I will always have time for you."

She smiled and hugged him around the neck. *I'm sorry for being rude.*

Late that night, after they'd gone home, Shreve lay in bed stroking Sabra's arm, still dizzy and marveling at the change in his life. He hadn't told her about the baby. And after he'd loved her thoroughly, she was sleeping soundly on his chest. He thought his heart would burst. He swore he would do everything right and never take even a day of his life for granted. And he would be the best father any kid ever had, that was a must. He found he couldn't wait any longer. He kissed her forehead.

"Sabra, wake up."

"Hmm?" She nuzzled against him softly. "What is it? You want some more?"

He chuckled. "Always."

She yawned. "All right then." Her voice was still sleepy, and she rolled over on her back. "Do your worst."

"I think I already have."

She blinked, coming more awake. "Huh?"

He placed his hand on her stomach. "We're going to have a daughter."

Sabra sat up, now fully awake. "How would you know?"

"Tesla told me. She saw the baby inside you. We conceived her this afternoon."

She blinked a few times. "That's sooner than I anticipated…I…I don't know how I feel." She put her hands on her stomach, looking down and then back up at him. "Really?" A timid smile pulled at her lips.

"Really. I think we should name her Sophie."

Tears sprang to her eyes, and she sank back down against him, her head on his chest where it was before. "Damn, I love you, Shreve."

CHAPTER TWENTY ONE

Journey's hands trembled as she held the tesseract, approaching the Heart. The flames sparked around the top. She lay the cube on the ground and sat behind it, placing her hands flat on the dirt. The white light slid along the ground toward her, pooling under the cube for a moment and then stretching to her. It grabbed onto her hands.

So this is the blood lock? The heart asked inside her head with its ethereal voice.

"Yes. Will you accept it? Will you protect yourself and all of us from this coming threat?"

The Heart was silent. She held her breath, waiting for its answer. The light on the ground swirled around the cube and caressed the sides of it.

You may place it in the flames. I will generate the power to run it, but whether it ultimately works is no doing or fault of mine, but rests with those who created it... The girl, have her come to me... Alone.

"Yes. Thank you."

The light slid back, releasing Journey's hands. She picked the cube up and brought it to the flames. The flame reached out and enveloped the tesseract, taking it from her grasp. The cube held steady, suspended in the middle of the manifestation, as if it hung from an invisible wire.

Journey backed up and walked to where the rest of the group waited a distance away. All of their eyes were bright with anticipation for the news.

"The Heart has accepted the cube and will power the blood lock."

Everyone sighed in relief. Journey's eyes sought out Forest, her daughter clasped to her side.

"Tesla, the Heart wants to talk to you."

****

Tesla swallowed as she walked toward the flames, the fear of punishment, or worse, discovery, writhing in her stomach. How was she to talk to the Heart? Could it see her hands?

A voice came into her head, halting her in her tracks.

Don't be afraid of me, Tesla. I will keep your secret. You can answer me in your mind, the voice said.

She clenched her hands together. *What secret?* She thought.

Hope is an important element to survival. You've given them that. But you and I know the blood lock will not hold for long. You have deceived them very skillfully. Even the two others who created the lock with you don't know.

I'm not finished, Tesla insisted. *I just haven't yet found what I need to make it what the others believe it to be. I've been searching other worlds. I know the answer is out there, somewhere.*

A terrible crashing noise tore through the sky. Tesla cowered, covering her ears, as the first alarm Merhl put in place was tripped. She rushed forward, reaching into the flames, opening the tesseract and turning it on. A blood red shockwave shot out from the cube, stretching over the whole of Regia. The barrier solidified on the tail of the shockwave.

The flames sparked. *You better hurry, girl. I will use what you've made to hold them back as best I can, but they are coming, and they will crash against this wall like the ocean.*

THE END

Don't miss out on the action, adventure, and romance of the final book in **The Legends of Regia** series,

Lightning Flower.

Coming Fall 2016!

ABOUT THE AUTHOR

Nationally Bestselling author Tenaya Jayne has always walked a shaky line between reality and fantasy. A nomad by nature, she's lived all over the US, and now resides happily in the Midwest, with her husband and sons. She's an advocate for Autism awareness and women trapped in abusive relationships, and feels everyone has too much pain to not enjoy an escape into a fictional fantasy world. Her passions include reading, independent and foreign films, cooking, and moody music. For more about Tenaya and her books, visit www.tenayajayne.com

www.ingramcontent.com/pod-product-compliance
Lightning Source LLC
Chambersburg PA
CBHW031949170626
46807CB00006B/2417